An Extraordinary Christmas

Seven Heartwarming Short Stories

Leslie Allebach

Paperback ISBN: 979-8-9872064-1-6
Ebook ISBN: 979-8-9872064-0-9

Table of Contents

The Candle
in the Window

Helen's uncooperative hands shook as she struck the match against its box. It took three tries before the match and the box finally connected. The warm flame wobbled as her hand stretched towards the simple red pillar candle that sat surrounded by a plastic holly candle ring in the deep sill of the front window. As the match brought the wick of the candle to life, Helen's heart was filled with an odd and comfortable nostalgia. She hobbled to her recliner and sat down with a deep sigh.

Alone. Always alone. The loneliness was especially painful at Christmastime. It had been five years now. Thoughts of Roy, her husband of fifty-five years, brought a smile. They had been through so much together. Until a massive heart attack had ended his life one cold, blustery day in January. Oh, how Helen wished she had died first. Instead, she was left to roam this house and find something to do, day after day, month after month, year after lonely year. The past year had been especially lonely as her worsening arthritis limited her activities severely.

8

Her friend, Marge, wasn't lonely. Oh, how she envied her! Her children and grandchildren visited regularly, taking her to special restaurants and beautiful gardens and church concerts. Great-grandchildren danced and played around her feet, calling her "Granny". Helen couldn't help but compare all of this to her too-quiet life. Once in a while, Marge invited her to a family outing. But this inevitably reminded Helen of all that she was missing and so she generally refused Marge's offers.

Unbidden, thoughts of Kenneth filled her mind. Her precious boy. What would her life have been like if Kenneth had come home from Canada? Would she have grandchildren and great-grandchildren? Or would his teen-aged rebellion have led him to completely sever ties with his parents forever?

She would never know. That is probably what ate at her soul the most. *She would never know.*

Kenneth would be close to 70 now if he were alive. Her heart would still fill with shame, even after all of these years, when she remembered the circumstances of her pregnancy. She remembered the dismay of being unwed and pregnant at 16, the love that she and Roy had shared even as teenagers, and the hurried wedding they were forced into at an all-too-young age. It had all worked out, although her father had never really forgiven her for bringing such dishonor to the family name.

After they were married, Helen fully expected her home to be filled with happy children. She waited excitedly for the siblings that would join Kenneth. But as the years came and went, her hopes for a large family started to dwindle. When Kenneth was six years old, there was the excitement of a pregnancy, but hopes were dashed almost before they took root when she miscarried at twelve weeks. Helen never got pregnant again.

From that time on, all of her mother's love and energy were poured into the little boy that had resulted from an unwanted pregnancy. The happy little youngster had been so kind and thoughtful, always thinking of others. And smart! He was smart as a whip! Helen remembered proudly. But in the turmoil of the sixties, dear Kenny had taken up with some friends who were not a very good influence. He started growing his hair, using marijuana, and became an outspoken protester of the Vietnam War. As Helen struggled to communicate and discuss the issues with their son, Roy, on the other hand, was just furious. One crisp autumn day, he had finally told Kenny that if he was going to turn his back on his country, then he was turning his back on his family and was no longer welcome to stay in their home.

Helen could still remember Kenny angrily packing his things and carrying them out to his beat-up VW van. As he shoved and stuffed it full of all of his earthly belongings, she had pleaded with him to stay. When he had brusquely told her to get out of his way, she had gone to find Roy, who was sitting in stone silence in his recliner, staring blankly at the evening news on the black and white TV. Roy, too, had ignored her pleas and within an hour, Kenneth had driven off towards the sun that was setting on the horizon.

Helen had spent the next weeks in despair. Where was their boy? And how would she ever be able to forgive Roy for driving their son away? Even now, all these years later, Helen wondered if she had ever truly forgiven him. The pain, buried under other memories now, still plagued her sometimes.

Somehow the couple had learned to live with their new normal. Each new day was just a bit easier than the one before and within a year of Kenny's departure Helen and Roy had reached a truce of sorts. They were fine, as long as the subject of Kenneth wasn't raised.

During that time, Helen longed to hear something— anything— from her son, but nary a word came. Until that fateful day.

Oh, how she hated that day.

Eddy, Kenny's best friend during that tumultuous time, had knocked on their door about two years after the departure. Roy was at work at the time. As Eddy stood at the door, nervously pulling at his scruffy beard, Helen could see that he was visibly upset. She invited him in and offered him a cup of coffee. He said no thanks and, without even sitting down, proceeded to tell her that Kenneth had been killed in a car accident a month before. He and Eddy had moved to Canada to avoid the draft and one snowy evening the boys were on their way back from the grocery store when they had hit a slick spot and slid off the road and into a tree. Eddy had escaped with just a few bruises but Kenneth had been killed on impact.

Helen had stood there shocked. So this was how it was all to end? Her beloved son was gone from this earth for forever?

Even now, all these years later, Helen's eyes filled with tears. They started to trickle down her weathered face. She drew comfort from the red candle, one of Kenneth's favorite boyhood traditions of Christmas. They would light a red candle in the window each holiday season to symbolize the light Jesus had brought to the world at Christmastime.

Reminiscing always tired Helen and after an hour she pulled her old body up out of her chair, blew out the candle, and went to bed.

Jessa stared at her tanned skin and thick, curly hair in the mirror. It was a strange thing—this being part black and part white. Which world did she belong to? Even as a 50-year-old, she still didn't really know. She washed her face and brushed her teeth as she pondered this question that had resided somewhere in the back of her mind for her whole life.

A few moments later found her staring at the contents of her closet. What does one wear to their mother's funeral? She found her favorite black sweater and looked it over. This? She dropped the sleeve of the sweater and lifted the hanger of a black and gray print shirt. Or this?

Finally settling on a pair of flattering black trousers and the print shirt, she started to put on her favorite heels. And then she remembered that this day would mean being on her feet for many hours. She put her heels back on the shoe rack and reached for her black flats instead.

"Logan? Lacey? You ready to go?" She called her 15-year-old son and 13-year-old daughter as she walked out of her room.

Mark, her husband, met her downstairs and gave her a warm embrace, "I'm so sorry, honey. I know how hard this is."

Jessa felt her eyes start to burn at his kind words. She quickly swiped at her eyes. She couldn't start crying already. The funeral hadn't even begun.

Ten long hours later, they came home exhausted after a long day of talking to people who had loved Bernadette Williams, lovingly called Grandma Nettie by almost all who knew her.

As they sat down in the family room, Logan and Lacey started talking about Aunt Althea's crushing hugs. Althea, Grandma Nettie's youngest sister, was a large, matronly woman who loved on others by wrapping them in her arms and squeezing them tight. The family started laughing, which was a welcome relief from the many tears that had been shed that day.

Nettie had had a very short battle with cancer and her family was still in shock over her quick departure from this earth. However, her vibrant relationship with her Heavenly Father and her faith in Jesus Christ alone for salvation gave them calm assurance that they would most certainly see her again.

They continued to talk about memories of Grandma Nettie when, out of the blue, Lacey turned to her mother with an unexpected question.

"Mom, whatever happened to your dad?"

Jessa was rather surprised that Lacey hadn't asked this question before. She remembered having a conversation about this with Logan when he was around the same age and she answered her the same way she had answered Logan, "He died before I was born."

"Oh."

Jessa figured that was the end of it. But Lacey had another question.

"Have you ever tried to find his family? Wouldn't it be so cool to meet them and see what they look like?" Lacey's eyes lit up as she pondered the excitement of solving a lifelong mystery. This was so typical of Lacey. Always dreaming about possibilities and ever passionate about solving mysteries.

It wasn't like Jessa had never considered it before. Once, when she was seventeen, she and her mother had had a long talk about it. Nettie had given her blessing for Jessa to search for her dad's family but something had held her back. Perhaps it was the knowledge that her father had left his family under bad terms. Whatever it was, she had decided at that time to just be content with her life the way it was. Until today. Until Lacey's question.

Perhaps it was because Jess was now truly an orphan—both her mother and father were gone. It made her feel empty. Honestly, this whole day was making her feel a little unsettled inside. She gave a deep sigh. Funny how a question from a 13-year-old can change everything.

Marge tapped her fingers impatiently on her kitchen counter as she waited for Helen to pick up the phone. Marge and Helen had been friends for a long time, but they couldn't be more opposite. Helen, quiet and frail, was often eclipsed by blustery, outspoken Marge who was thin as a rail, healthy as a horse, and still sharp as a tack.

"Hello?" Helen had finally answered.

"Helen? Are you okay? It took you awhile to get to the phone," shouted Marge into the receiver.

"I'm fine, Marge. The phone was on the other side of the room and I don't move as quickly these days," Helen reminded her.

"Yeah, yeah, I know what you mean," Marge said, even though she really didn't have any idea what she meant. She continued, "So I am calling to find out if you want to come along to Brenda's this Christmas Eve? We'd really like you to come."

Brenda, Marge's daughter, had the entire family at her home every Christmas Eve. It was full of laughter and fun and joy. And Helen hated it.

Several years ago, she had finally told Marge she would go along with her. A few minutes into the evening she knew she would never go again. As she had sat there alone watching the children play together and listening to the conversations around her it was just a fresh reminder that she didn't really belong anywhere.

"Helen! You still there?" asked Marge, a little impatiently.

Marge's question brought Helen's mind back to the present. She quickly came up with an excuse, just as she did every year, "Aw, Marge, thanks so much for asking me. Unfortunately, with this damp weather, my arthritis has been really acting up lately. I'd better just stay home."

"Okay, Helen Rose Morgan, if that is the way you want it," Marge always used Helen's full name when she was a bit perturbed with her. But, while she was a little irritated, she certainly wasn't surprised at Helen's refusal to join them. Lame excuses were what she had come to expect. It still saddened her that her friend would be all alone on Christmas Eve and so Marge decided that this year she wouldn't let that happen. She continued after a brief moment, "How about I eat dinner with my family and then come to your house afterward? It might be kind of nice to have a quiet Christmas Eve for a change," Marge spoke the words even though she didn't mean them.

"Are you sure, Marge? I wouldn't want to..."

"Of course, I'm sure."

Helen responded with a grateful sigh, "thank you, Marge. I would like that."

The two friends spent the next few moments on the phone talking about what Christmas movie they would watch that night. Marge liked *What a Wonderful Life* and Helen's favorite was *Christmas in Connecticut*. Finally, Marge laughed and said, "Let's watch both!"

And so the plans were made. A little smile tugged at the corners of Helen's mouth as she hung up the phone.

She sat down at her Formica kitchen table for a few moments and basked in the warm glow that came at the thought of not having to spend Christmas Eve alone this year. It was a very odd thing–this being without any living relatives. Her husband had been an only child and so there were no relatives on that side of the family except for a few distant cousins. Helen had had a sister,

15

Ida Jane, but she had never married and had died suddenly in her 40s. It all seemed so long ago now. Time had passed and gradually dulled the emptiness of it all and Helen had grown quite used to not having a family. In fact, most times it didn't bother her. Except for this time of year. What was it about having family around at Christmas?

The lurking shadow of loneliness dissipated as she shook her head to clear the old memories away and determined to have a good attitude. After all, this year she didn't have to spend Christmas Eve alone! She tuned the radio to a station playing Christmas carols and hummed along as she washed the dishes.

Jessa carefully pulled the thick red candle from its tissue wrapping. A plastic holly candle ring, already unwrapped, lay on the floor beside her. As she held the candle, she could feel tears burn behind her eyes. Willing herself not to cry, she tenderly placed the candle on a glass plate and placed the holly ring over it. As she set it gently on the table in front of the main family room window, one lone tear spilled over and made its way down her cheek.

Unpacking the memories of Christmases long past was a heart-breaking affair. Her mother had loved Christmas. There were five boxes of beautiful, albeit tacky, Christmas decorations to prove it. Looking at the remaining boxes, Jessa thought it might be wise to wait until the kids got home from school to go through them. Their chatter would be a welcome distraction.

She went to the kitchen and made a cup of coffee. She eyed the plate filled with Christmas cookies on the counter and then picked up a couple of them and placed them on a napkin. Taking her coffee and cookies back to the family room, she sat down in a comfortable chair and picked up the novel that she was currently reading. Perhaps immersing herself within its pages would take her mind off of just how much she missed her mom.

A few minutes later, she sighed and closed her book. She had just read the same page four times. Putting the book on the table beside her, she sat munching on a cookie. Childhood memories of her mother and Christmases long past flooded her mind. Mother and daughter had weathered many trials as a team and the bond between them had been strong. Christmas had always been a happy break from the hard times and Jessa was so thankful for the memories. However, reviewing them was painful and the fact that her mom had died just a few weeks before the holiday wasn't making it any easier.

Her eyes fell on the red candle. They had had Christmases without a Christmas tree. They had gone without turkeys and wreaths and gingerbread and presents. But they never had a Christmas without that red candle in the window.

The candle reminded her of her father. She had never met him but the red candle in the window had always been placed there in his honor. Her mother had told Jessa that the candle was one of her father's favorite Christmas traditions from his childhood home and how the young couple had gone to the local Woolworth's to buy their first bright red candle and cheap plastic ring of holly. It was the only Christmas decoration her parents could afford to buy that first and only Christmas together as a married couple.

What had her father been like? She had seen a photo or two but photos told so very little. Nettie had told Jessa that she felt like she never really knew the man her father would have become as he grew in the Lord. Nettie had often shared the story with Jessa of how she had married an unbeliever and counseled her daughter not to follow in her footsteps. But she had rejoiced that God had saved him! Oh, how she rejoiced! Especially since he was gone a few short weeks later. And Nettie would then tell her daughter how her father had repented of his sins and accepted Jesus Christ as his personal Savior just before the tragic car accident that took his life. She told Jessa that after her father was saved, he had stopped drinking with his friends and how grateful she was for those few precious weeks of happy memories.

Jessa knew little else about him—except that he was a white man from New York. And that his name was Kenneth. *Kenneth Roy Morgan.*

Helen lit the red candle and then went into the kitchen to heat up the leftover Christmas dinner that Marge had brought her last night. The memory of the night before warmed her heart. Christmas Eve spent with a friend was so much better than spending it alone. It even took a bit of the sting out of spending Christmas Day all by herself. She hummed *Joy to the World* as the microwave heated her meal.

She decided to take the plate of the food into the living room. This was the last evening that she would burn the Christmas Candle and she wanted to fully enjoy it. Setting the plate on her recliner seat, she pulled an old TV tray table from its spot in the corner and set it up. She sat and rested for a minute or two before turning on the TV and digging into the turkey and stuffing before her.

Thirty minutes later found her dozing, with an empty plate in front of her and an old Christmas movie playing on the TV.

Helen had no idea that just outside her door stood a family that would change her life forever.

Jessa licked her lips nervously. Perhaps this was a really crazy idea. Maybe her grandmother wouldn't even want to see her. *What was she thinking?*

"Ready?" Mark smiled at her.

Lacey was full of nervous excitement, while Logan looked just a bit bored at the whole situation.

"Okay, let's do this," Jessa determinedly started walking towards the front door of the little white Cape Cod. When the rest of the family had gathered there with her, she took a deep breath and then knocked.

Since setting out the red candle at home a few weeks ago, Jessa had felt an increasing desire to find out if anyone from her father's family was still alive. What she had discovered was that there was only one person to meet—her father's elderly mother. The family had decided they would drive the hour south across the border to visit her after they had had Christmas dinner with her mother's side of the family. Jessa had reflected on how her father had settled so close to home when he left as a young man. How different her life would have been had he lived.

Since they had been with Mark's family on Christmas Eve, Christmas evening had seemed like the perfect time to make the momentous visit. But now they were here. At her house. On Christmas day. To Jessa it all felt quite surreal and a bit frightening.

Mark, with supportive arm around Jessa, leaned over to press the doorbell and then gave a firm knock on the door, just in case.

As the family stood on the front porch and waited, they looked around. The little house was in much disrepair. Besides being in dire need of a fresh coat of paint, the porch was rotting away and the shrubbery needed trimmed. Mark, always big-hearted and

19

generous, started thinking about how the family could help his wife's grandmother before he even met her.

Suddenly, the door swung open, and there stood a small, thin woman.

"Merry Christmas to you," Jessa said nervously, "are you Mrs. Helen Morgan? Helen Rose Morgan?"

"Why yes, that's me," she said, puzzled. She shivered as a gust of cold air blew into the warm room behind her.

"We are the Washington family and we have come from across the border to see you. May we come in for just a moment? We have something we'd like to share with you."

Helen grew just a little nervous at the smiling strangers. Her eyes took in the tall African-American man with glasses and then moved to the pretty tan blue-eyed woman with dark curly hair. With them were two older children. The boy looked like he didn't want to be there but the girl looked sweet. *Who in the world would come visiting a stranger on Christmas day? How odd!* She stared at them for a few more seconds before finally deciding they looked safe enough and inviting them inside.

"Have a seat," she said as she gestured to the sofa across the room. Her hands shook nervously as she second-guessed the wisdom of letting strangers into her home. She had heard horrible stories about wicked people who tricked and terrorized the elderly. What if they were going to steal from her? Or, even worse, kill her?

There must have been a look of terror in her eyes, for Mark tenderly touched her shoulder and said, "Oh, Mrs. Morgan, you need not fear. We are here to share good news!"

He moved to the slip-covered sofa and sat down. The family followed his lead and soon they were all

20

squeezed there, side by side. Helen felt herself relax just a bit. They did look like a nice, normal family.

After they introduced themselves, they all sat there for a few awkward moments in silence, until finally Mark gave an imperceptible nod of his head to Jessa. At that, Jessa said a quick prayer for strength and then just decided to get it over with. Out it all came in one big rush, "Mrs. Morgan, we are here because, well, I think you are my grandmother."

Helen's eyes grew big at this but she remained quiet.

"You see, my father died in a car accident before I was born so I never met him. I knew his name was Kenneth Roy Morgan and thought about trying to find his family through the years but..."

"Your father was Kenneth Roy Morgan?" Helen interrupted, aghast, "Are you sure? Kenny didn't have any children."

As Jessa shared her story of how Kenny and Bernadette had met and then got married and had her, Helen started shaking uncontrollably.

"Kenny's daughter? You are Kenny's daughter?" Helen kept saying it over and over again in disbelief.

"Are you okay, Grandma?" Lacey rushed to her side in her typical fashion. To this precocious and loving child, this woman was her grandma and it made total sense to call her that. She had no idea that this name was a name that Helen never thought she would be called. The shock was almost too much.

Mark stepped in, "Lacey would you go to the kitchen and get Mrs. Morgan a glass of water?"

As she left to do her father's bidding, he tenderly held Helen's hand, "Mrs. Morgan, we are so sorry for the shock. A few weeks ago, Jessa's mother died. This event awakened in her a desire to find her father's family. As she searched, she realized that you are the only relative left on her father's side. She wanted to meet you as soon as possible and so here we are. Are you okay?"

Helen's heart had stopped pounding as this new and wonderful thought started to seep into her brain and then settled into her heart. She had a family! She had a FAMILY! *SHE HAD A FAMILY!* The words just kept ringing in her ears.

Happy tears made their way down her wrinkled face as unfamiliar hope started to grow in her heart. As she sipped the cup of water Lacey handed her, she looked at Jessa. She had felt like something was familiar about the woman but couldn't figure out what. But suddenly, she knew! It was her distinct bluish-green eyes. Kenneth had those same eyes. And the boy–Jessa's son—he looked like Kenneth. How had she missed that earlier? Oh, he had darker skin but he had those same eyes and something about his face reminded her of her boy at that age. She knew without a doubt that this family was telling her the truth.

"Come here, dear," Helen directed the gentle request to Jessa. When Jessa was kneeling in front of her, Helen put her frail hand up to caress her face, "Oh, how much I have missed. Oh, how dreadfully sorry I am that I wasn't there for you and your mother. If only I had known," she said sadly and then sat in silence for a few moments while Jessa tenderly held her hand and then Helen smiled and looked at the children, "So I suppose that makes you two my great-grandchildren!" she said with a twinkle in her eye.

Logan gave a gentle smile—even he was affected by this reunion– but Lacey jumped to her feet and rushed to her great-grandmother's side, talking a mile a minute, "So what would you like me to call you, Grandma? I mean, I know that you aren't really my grandma, but "great-grandma" seems like such a long name to call you and since my other grandma just died, maybe you could kinda take her place? Well, not take her place exactly but be my grandma now that she's gone? Would that be okay?—", she was prepared to go on but Mark quickly put a firm hand on her shoulder.

"Shhh, Lacey," he said quietly behind her.

"Oh, don't shush her," said Helen merrily, "I haven't had this much fun since—well, perhaps since your father left our home," this she directed to Jessa, "It has been an awfully long time since I had some young blood around here and I am enjoying it immensely!"

And, with that, she turned towards Lacey and the two of them chatted on and on, while the rest of the family watched with amused expressions and happy hearts.

A little later in the evening, Mark asked if he could read the Christmas story and the family talked about God's Son coming in a manger and how He would later grow up to die so that man could be forgiven and reconciled to God. They talked about Jesus like He was their friend. Helen was puzzled about this Jesus and unfamiliar with the details surrounding Him, as written in scripture. To her, He was just part of her Christmas tradition. Nothing more, nothing less.

A few hours later, the family gathered their things together with a promise to return soon. Phone numbers were exchanged and Jessa promised to call Helen and check on her the next day. The family all hugged Helen good-bye like they had known her for years. Their coats were on and they were just about to leave when Jessa stopped in her tracks as she spotted the red candle.

"That candle in the window..."

"Oh, yes, that was one of your father's favorite Christmas traditions!" smiled Helen, "Light a red candle to..."

"Symbolize the light that Jesus brought to the world," finished Jessa, "My mom and I did that in honor of my dad for all of my growing up years. In fact, I am continuing the tradition at my house now."

Helen's heart felt like it would burst. Kenny's memory was still alive in another heart besides her own. It was so comforting somehow.

With promises to return again soon and a few more hugs, they were gone and the house grew strangely quiet again. Helen sat back down in her recliner with just the candle for light and reveled in pleasant thoughts of summer picnics and family dinners. She dreamed of going to gardens and concerts with her new family. And, most of all, of never having to spend another Christmas alone. After an hour of daydreaming, she blew out the candle in the window and went to bed.

In the months and years to follow, Helen's newfound family would fulfill all their promises and more to the elderly lady. There were many summer picnics and family dinners. They took her to concerts and gardens. And Helen never spent another Christmas alone but was, instead, surrounded by her loving family. But, most of all, they introduced her to the baby in a manger. They told her that Jesus had died for her sins and that if she believed on Him as her Savior, she would be reconciled to God and spend eternity with Him in Heaven.

Helen did believe and started studying her Bible during her many hours alone. Placing the red candle in the window each Christmas became even more special as Helen finally understood the real meaning of the long-held family tradition.

And when, five years later, she slipped away quietly in her sleep, her family knew, without a shadow of a doubt, that they would see her again.

Meeting Ella

I approached the front door with a combination of fear and nostalgia, the wind whipping my hair into my eyes. The front of the big farm house looked so forlorn. The last time I was here it had been Christmastime. Garland with twinkling white lights had hung over the door. Big red pots that held miniature Christmas trees had sat like guards on each side of the steps. And out in the lawn had been the wooden nativity made by my Uncle Gus.

I sighed with sadness as I pulled the key out of my coat pocket and placed it into the deadbolt on the door. What a difference a year can make.

Had it only been six months since Gram had died? It felt so much longer than that--and so much shorter. When my parents had died in a car accident when I was just a baby, my grandparents had raised me. Grandpa had died two years ago and my Uncle Gus a year before that. And now Gram.

I pushed in the big wooden door and hesitantly stepped inside to the entry way. The stale smell of an unlived-in house assaulted my nose. I walked through the familiar rooms downstairs, pulling sheets off the furniture amidst clouds of dust.

I had called the utility companies last week to assure I would have electric and water when I arrived. Tomorrow I'd call about setting up wifi.

I ended up in the kitchen, where I plugged in the refrigerator and stove and pushed them back to the wall, relieved to hear the hum of the refrigerator as it started up.

The magnitude of what I was doing suddenly hit me. *What I had gotten myself into?*

As Gram's only living relative, I had inherited the house. My first thought had been to put it on the market immediately. But there was something that held me back. Maybe it was the memories. After all, it was the only home I had ever known.

I decided to give myself a few months to think about it and during that time I had lost my graphic design job when the small company I worked for was bought by a larger company.

I remembered the conversation well. *We are sorry, Libby. We value your talent and wish we could keep you but the other company already has a designer on staff and we don't need two. Please feel free to ask us for a recommendation. We wish you the best.*

And that was that. I had worked two more weeks and then took my small severance package, packed up my office, and walked out the door.

But what had seemed devastating at the time started to look like the purpose of God leading me back to this house. My job was the main thing holding me back from moving. Now I didn't have any excuses left.

And so, I had sold my furniture, packed up what was left in my Jeep Cherokee, and traveled across the state to my hometown. And here I was on a cold, windy night in December.

I shouldn't have come back at Christmastime. I realized that now. Anytime would have been difficult but December was by far the worst. Gram had loved Christmas. It had been the most special time of the year. Even last year, when she was really slowing down due to her heart failure, I had hauled the boxes out of the attic and she had sat, her knees covered with a bright red afghan, and directed me with her smiley face and twinkly eyes.

I sat down on a kitchen chair and laid my head on my arms. My shoulders started to shake. Christmas would never be the same again. Never.

I must have sat there for fifteen minutes, sobbing, when suddenly I got the distinct impression that someone was watching me. My eyes scanned the nearby doorway and then moved around the room. I didn't see anyone. I wiped my face on my sleeve, stood up, and looked around a bit before chalking it up to my imagination.

I shrugged and decided to head upstairs, eager to see my old bedroom. As I walked up the creaky stairs, the strangeness and unfamiliarity of being in this big old house by myself assailed me. It was not a pleasant feeling. But I had sold everything now and didn't have much of a choice but to stay here. At least for a little while, as I decided what to do next.

I found my bedroom very much like I had left it, which I found comforting. I sat down on the edge of my bed and sighed. I was home. Even without Gram, it felt like home.

This feeling renewed my energy and I jumped from the bed to go get my stuff. I glanced in some of the other bedrooms on the way, just for old times' sake.

Uncle Gus's room still had the plaid bedspread and dark oak furniture. And there was Gram's room with the delicate floral wallpaper. I checked out the guest room, made up with one of Gram's brightly colored quilts. And then, finally, headed down to the last tiny room on the right. I remembered that this room held a twin bed and Gram's sewing machine. It was one of my favorite rooms in the house and I had spent many hours playing on the floor with my puzzles and dolls while she sewed and quilted there.

However, I was not prepared for what I found in that room. The bed looked like it had been slept in the night before, unmade and unkempt. There was a small cup of water by the bedside, along with a girl's sweater. I picked up the purple sweater and stared at it. It was a size 10, faded, with a tear at the elbow.

Questions came to me in rapid succession. Had Gram had a young visitor here when she died? And who in the world had it been? And where was she now? And why hadn't Gram bought her a new sweater?

Oh, well. Those were questions for another day. For now, I needed to go get my stuff and move in. I ran lightly down the stairs and out to my car, ready to unload my things. Tomorrow I would get out the Christmas decorations. It was a good day. I was home.

By 7pm, the big house was feeling a bit more like my old home. I had even dusted and swept. I sighed with contentment. The fond memories of this place filled me with a peace I hadn't known for quite some time. Of course, there was a big empty hole without Gram here. And something else was missing, too.

What was it?

I walked through the house and made my way to the living room. Spotting the braided rug in front of the hearth, it came to me. It was Snoopy. It was just not the same here without the little black dog that used to follow me around everywhere I went.

With the flip of a switch a fire came to life in the fireplace insert Uncle Gus and I had talked Gram into buying awhile back. The comfortable overstuffed blue chair by the stone hearth was the perfect place to do a little day dreaming. I allowed my mind to travel back in time to that moment when Gram had finally allowed me to get a dog. Driving to the local shelter and giddy with excitement, I had found the happiest puppy there and named him Snoopy—after my favorite cartoon dog.

From the beginning, our relationship was special. We became fast friends and were inseparable. I was heart-broken when he died during my freshman year of college. I had longed for another dog ever since, but apartment living and a demanding job just didn't make it possible. Of course, all that had changed now.

Wait! Yes, all that had changed! What was holding me back? I grew excited as I considered the prospect of owning a dog again. In fact, I could feasibly go back to that same shelter and find a new dog. What quicker way was there to shoo away the loneliness of this house than with a new canine friend? Tomorrow grew into an exciting adventure as I pondered this idea.

I was jolted back to reality as my mind turned to my job situation. That was of grave concern. I didn't need to worry about it for a few months but those months would go by fast. I shook my head, as if to free it of the troublesome thoughts and grabbed my keys. That problem would have to wait until tomorrow as I had a much more important priority currently—a grumbling belly that was urging me to eat.

I drove into town and pulled into Martha's Diner. As I munched on a hamburger and fries, I looked around, hoping to see a familiar face but saw not a one. It had been over ten years since I had lived in the area. I realized that things change a lot in that amount of time.

Feeling rather lonely and out-of-place, I pulled out my iPhone and started scrolling through Facebook. The happy faces of my city friends provided a sobering reminder of all that I had given up.

Photos of adorable children and beautifully decorated homes reminded me that I didn't fit in with my married friends, either. In fact, I didn't really fit into any world at the moment. It was rather disconcerting.

"Libby? Libby Barnwell?"

I glanced up to see a smiling, older couple staring at me.

"Mr. and Mrs. Miller? How nice to see you," I gave the older lady a warm hug and then turned to Mr. Miller to shake his hand, but, he, too, pulled me into a big hug.

This couple, dear friends of my Gram, provided just the dose of encouragement I needed. We chatted for several minutes about life and change and then they made me promise that I would be at church on Sunday.

"We will save you a seat, dear. We always sit about six rows back on the right and will look for you. And please plan on having lunch with us afterward. Our granddaughter, Katie, is living with us currently and I think you two would really get along. Don't you think so, Jim? She's in grad school at the local university so she is living with us for a while," explained Mrs. Miller. And then with one final hug, they walked out of the diner.

Thank you, Lord. Thank you for bringing a familiar face. That was exactly what I needed.

I had one last cup of coffee and then paid my bill. Glancing at my watch, I saw that I had time to run by the grocery store to pick up a few things. My trip to the store didn't take very long and soon I was back at home unloading my car in the bitter wind. Dropping the last bag on the table and locking the door behind me, I reached up to feel my cold cheeks. Winter had certainly arrived.

I quickly put everything away and then checked the clock above the sink. Only 9:30pm. The sound of the wind drew me to take refuge in my comfortable, childhood bed and so, grabbing a book from my backpack, I made my way upstairs and got ready for bed. I snuggled down into the blankets and down comforter and then sniffed. These would definitely need a good airing tomorrow.

Engrossed in my book a few minutes later, I froze when, suddenly, I heard a creak coming from the direction of the stairs.

I strained to hear anything further, but nothing came. After what seemed like hours (but was probably only a few minutes), I returned to my book. Wait! There it was again! Someone was definitely in this house. I immediately realized my vulnerable situation. No weapons. No friends. No family. I was quite defenseless. I didn't even know a phone number of a neighbor, for goodness' sake.

I started to panic. I tried to calm myself by remembering that old houses make noises. It was windy tonight. It was probably just the wind.

I lay there for a few more minutes but couldn't shake the idea that someone was in the house. I decided to go check. Anything was better than laying in my bed paralyzed in fear. I glanced around for some kind of weapon. The only thing I spotted was a small glass candlestick on the dresser. I picked it up and held it in front of me with one hand and opened the door with the other. I must have made quite a site, me tiptoeing quietly across the room in my snowflake print pajamas, polka-dot slippers, and carrying a glass candlestick as my only source of protection against who knew what?

I peeked out of my room and looked both ways. Nothing. I cautiously stepped out into the hallway. I crept down the stairs and explored the first level. It didn't seem as if anything had been disturbed. I hesitated at the cellar door. Even in the daytime, I hated the cellar. But I knew I wouldn't be able to sleep if I didn't check it out and so I opened the door, switched on the light, and started down the steps. Halfway down the L-shaped steps was a window that stood wide open. Each gust of wind would cause it to move and creak just a bit.

An open window would definitely cause strange noises on a windy night. I sighed with relief and quickly shut and locked it. From my vantage point of the steps, I looked around the forgotten room. It was piled high with Gram's stuff and someone could easily hide there. This thought gave me no comfort.

At that point, I realized that I had a decision to make. I could either trust the Lord to take care of me or I could choose to be fearful. God and I had a close relationship. He had saved me from my sins and He promised to care for me. My job was to trust Him and not cave in to fear.

With a prayer for protection, I headed back to bed, trusting that He would keep me safe through the night.

A few minutes later I was tucked under the stale-smelling covers and, after an hour or two of lying there listening to the strange noises an old house makes at night, I finally drifted off into a troubled sleep.

Morning came far too quickly after my restless night. Dragging myself out of bed, I got ready for the day and then made myself some toast. Last night's events played through my mind as I ate my breakfast and, thankfully, my fears were considerably diminished in the bright morning sunshine. *Of course, houses make strange*

noises—especially hundred-year-old farm houses, I told myself. I would just have to get used to it.

Perhaps a dog would help. It was so disconcerting being in this house completely alone, especially at night. I put my dishes in the sink and grabbed my coat, excited for today's adventure.

The first stop was the local Walmart to buy some pet supplies. The brightly colored collars and leashes drew my eye. I picked out a medium-sized, green polka-dotted collar, with a leash to match. That seemed to be the safest selection, as it could be used for a male or female medium-sized dog.

My cart was soon loaded with dog food, dog treats, bowls, pet shampoo, and a big, over-sized dog bed. I walked by the crates and realized that this was probably going to be a necessity, as well. Who knew how well-behaved this dog would be? And so, a medium-sized crate went in on top of everything else. I carefully wheeled my cart to the front and through the checkout. I watched as the items began to add up to an exorbitant amount. Shopping sprees like this would have to be extremely rare these next few months.

A half hour later, I was walking through the concrete hallways of the local shelter. There was certainly no dearth of dogs from which to choose. There were big ones and small ones, ferocious ones and friendly ones. How would I ever choose just one?

And then I saw him. He sat calmly in the corner of his cage but as I approached his tail started wagging fiercely. He greeted me like a perfect gentleman—happily but without that over-the-top excitement that some dogs have. Short brown hair with a small white patch on his chest and medium-sized, I knew he was just right for me. His name was Buddy and it suited him perfectly. Buddy it was.

Soon all of the paperwork was signed, the small fee was paid, and we were on our way home. Buddy was amazing right from the start. He sat quietly in the car looking out the window.

As the car pulled into the driveway, Buddy's tail started wagging as if to say "What an adventure!" He hopped out and excitedly started to explore his new home. He followed me into the house and happily continued his exploration. Finally, he flopped down beside me in the kitchen to watch me prepare my lunch. His brown, soulful eyes silently asked me to share.

"Oh, alright!" I laughed as I threw a bit of cheese down to him.

After lunch, I decided to decorate for Christmas. Sure, only Buddy and I would really appreciate it, but somehow it just felt like the right thing to do. And so, turning the switch on at the bottom of the attic steps, up I went. Buddy followed me up the narrow stairway, sniffing all the way. It was clear that he was overjoyed with his newfound freedom. I found the Christmas decorations in the back right corner of the attic, just where I had put them last year and the year before that and, well, for forever. There were boxes upon boxes. Gram had certainly loved Christmas.

I opened the first box and found the tree decorations. I pushed that box towards the staircase. The second held Christmas-themed linens and tablecloths. Deeming them unnecessary, at least for this Christmas season, I pushed that one to the side. Continuing on in this manner for another thirty minutes, six boxes were soon waiting at the top of the stairs.

One by one, I lifted them and carried them downstairs to the dining room, almost tripping over Buddy a few times as he followed on my heels. But he was such a welcome addition to the house that I couldn't possibly grow angry with him so I just laughed and gently scolded him.

After all of the boxes were down, I made myself a cup of coffee and decided to sit down for a few minutes. My rough night soon caught up with me and I found myself dozing off. At least, until Buddy started barking at the sound of the doorbell. *Who could that be?* I peeked out the front window. Mrs. Miller stood there smiling, holding a candy-cane striped tin. Beside her stood a young woman with brown hair wearing a navy wool coat.

Opening the door, I welcomed them inside.

"Hello, dear! I hope we aren't bothering you. I just couldn't wait for you to meet my granddaughter. Kate, this is Libby. Libby, meet Kate. I am just sure you two will get along fabulously," She gestured eagerly from one to the other as we gave each other tentative—and rather awkward—smiles.

And then she continued, "And I just happened to do some baking this morning, so we brought some cookies along. They are the peanut butter kind with the Hershey Kisses on top. They are Jim's favorite," She winked as she handed me the tin and then started to look around, "Oh, so many memories here. We used to come and play games with your grandma. I sure do miss her."

And then she spotted the boxes of decorations in the dining room, "Oh! Did we interrupt you?"

"Well, I actually didn't get very far yet," I glanced at my watch and saw that it was already 3:30pm, "I will do what I can today and then finish tomorrow. There's really no big hurry. Can I get you some coffee?"

I saw Mrs. Miller turn to Katie and ask her a question before she turned back to me with a surprising question, "Libby, darling, could Katie and I help you decorate? We'd love to help and, besides, decorating by yourself is really not near as much fun as decorating with friends!" (She had such a warm and rather loud enthusiasm as she said this), "Kate assured me that she has a few spare hours. So why don't you go make coffee and put on some Christmas music and we will have ourselves a wonderful time. What do you say?"

Truth be told, I had really wanted to decorate alone. I wanted to take my time going through the old, familiar things and I wanted to be able to cry if I felt like crying. But Mrs. Miller was a force to be reckoned with and so, hiding my disappointment, I pasted on a smile and told her I'd love to have their help. I put on some Christmas music and then went to the kitchen and made three cups of hot coffee and put a few of the cookies from the tin on a plate. Buddy quietly stared at me and rubbed his nose on my legs as if to tell me he understood and was sorry for how things had turned out.

But, surprisingly, the next three hours flew by in a flurry of activity and merriment. First, we set up and decorated Gram's three artificial trees—The old-fashioned one in the living room; the formal one, bedecked with gold and silver, in the dining room; and the smallest one, decorated with simple bows and silk poinsettias, in the foyer. Next, we filled the banisters and mantel with green garland, white lights, gold stars, and tiny crocheted angels. I pulled Gram's collection of porcelain angels from their careful wrapping and set them around on every possible surface. Finally, we worked outside to put the garland and lights around the door. Kate had even helped me pull Uncle Gus's manger scene out of the old shed. I stood back with a great sense of satisfaction. Mrs. Miller was right—it had been so much more fun to accomplish this with friends.

Throughout the whole afternoon, Mrs. Miller was so wonderful—in both sharing snippets about Gram and also letting me reflect in silence at times. And she was right about Kate and me. We hit it off immediately. It felt like we had been friends our whole lives.

As I waved good-bye to them and went back inside, I smiled. I was so thankful for these new friends. Maybe it wouldn't be so bad here, after all. Kate and I had already made plans to go Christmas shopping together.

It was as I stood with my back against the closed door, thanking the Lord for His kind mercies to me, that I spotted it.

I squinted to be sure I saw it correctly. Under the dining room table was a small red mitten.

Where had that come from? It had definitely not been there when I vacuumed yesterday.

Picking it up and turning it over, I saw that it was a little girl's left mitten.

Startled, I began to suspect that the owner of the mitten and the owner of the purple sweater upstairs were probably the same little girl. And now I was beginning to wonder if the little owner might be in this house. That feeling of not being alone yesterday came to my mind. And, too, the odd open window last night. On a sudden hunch, I ran up the stairs to Gram's sewing room.

I was right. The purple sweater was gone and the rumpled covers on the bed were pulled up towards the pillow as if someone had tried to make it in a hurry. It became clear that I was not alone in this house.

As I stood there for a few moments wondering what to do, Buddy was wildly sniffing around the room, as if to confirm my suspicions.

My stomach growled, reminding me that it was long past dinnertime. I prepared a ham and cheese sandwich and put it on a plate with a handful of potato chips, all the while my ears listening for any possible sound. She had to be around here somewhere.

After dinner, I decided to go on an all-out hunt for this little person. I checked in closets, under beds, and behind dressers. Overcoming my fear, I looked in both the cellar and the attic, moving boxes and crates. I couldn't find anything. I didn't even see any more clues that would verify her existence. Perhaps I was just dreaming this all up. I remembered Mrs. Miller saying she taught Sunday School. Perhaps she had had the mitten in her coat pocket for some reason, I rationalized.

Feeling rather silly, I sat back down into the comfortable blue chair and turned on the TV. Soon I was engrossed in an old Christmas movie and forgot about my musings and speculations.

That is until Buddy started barking like crazy.

"Buddy! Stop!"

Maybe a dog wasn't such a good idea, after all. It was a little frightening to have a dog madly barking in an old house and having no idea why. I grabbed his collar and looked him the eye, "Stop!"

He didn't listen to me. In fact, he wriggled out of my grasp and ran to the cellar steps, growling and barking all the way.

I opened the door and he rushed past me, down into the darkness. Flipping the switch, I saw that the basement window was open once again. How had that happened?

And then I saw her. Standing at the bottom of the steps. She looked to be around nine. Soft, wheat-colored hair and pale skin. She had on a red wool coat that was stained and ripped at the hem and one red mitten. Tears welled up in her startlingly blue eyes as Buddy rushed at her.

"Aw, honey, don't cry," I shushed Buddy away and then sat down on the steps in front of her, helplessly uncertain as to what to do. A million questions danced through my mind, begging to be answered all at once.

I grabbed the girl's cold, mittenless left hand and gave it a warm squeeze, before softly asking, "What's your name?"

She took her mittened hand and rubbed it across her face to remove the tears that had started a quiet trail down her cheeks. She took a deep breath and then said faintly, "I'm Ella."

Ella. So this was who I had been sharing my house with for the past couple of days.

Ella sniffed a bit and then stared at me with her bright blue eyes. I felt completely out of my element. I had little experience with children and even less experience with such unexpected happenings like this. I gave her hand another warm squeeze and then dropped it and told her to follow me upstairs. Soon she was sitting at the table with a cup of hot cocoa and some of Mrs. Miller's cookies.

"So, Ella, how did you happen to choose my house to visit?" It seemed like a silly question but I didn't even know what else to ask. I didn't want to be too blunt, but I have to admit that curiosity was just about killing me by now. And she was so quiet. This did not look like it was going to be easy.

Should I call someone to help me? Should I take her somewhere? What does one do in a situation like this? I told myself to just relax and give her a moment.

She sat there a few more minutes, drinking cocoa and petting Buddy.

"What's his name?" she finally asked, ignoring my question.

"His name is Buddy. It suits him, I think. Do you agree?"

She soberly nodded and went back to her cocoa.

"So how did you get here, Ella?" I tried again.

With a catch in her throat, she started. She finally seemed ready to share and, with a few questions from me, she told me her whole story.

She had grown up with her single mom, Melanie, in a little town about an hour away. When Melanie had been diagnosed with terminal cancer, she had finally shared the story of Ella's father. She had told Ella how she had been lonely and sad, working in the office of a local mechanic. Thoughts of marriage had long since departed and her life was unexciting. One day, a handsome, older man had come to have his pick-up truck serviced. The two had hit it off immediately and were soon spending lots of time together.

Marriage was promised and so Melanie had let her guard down and soon became pregnant. But before she could let the man know he was going to be a father, he had disappeared out of her life, making it clear that it was over. She had resigned herself to her new life as a single mom and had made the best of it.

Little Ella had filled Melanie's life with love and sunshine, despite the circumstances of her birth. Melanie had always hoped deep down inside that the man would return and they could be a family but then a few years ago she had found out that the man had died. Melanie had cried when she told that part of the story to Ella and then had grown very serious as she had explained that she was not going to recover from her illness and Ella was going to need someone else to care for her. And, although Ella's father was no longer living, his mother—Ella's grandmother—was still alive and residing in a great big farmhouse all by herself.

Melanie, feeling alone and desperate, told Ella she was going to take her to her grandmother's house to live. She had met the woman a couple of times and she was quite confident that this was the best and safest place for Ella. Uncertain of what welcome she would receive as the mother of Gus's illegitimate child, Melanie had decided to carefully draft a note of explanation and had tucked it in an envelope along with Ella's birth certificate. Trying to spare her daughter the horror of watching her mother die and assuring her that her grandmother would be overjoyed to have her there, she had given Ella the envelope and simply dropped her off at the farm one Tuesday, without even so much as a knock on the door and drove away.

Unbeknownst to Melanie, Hattie Barnwell had passed away several months earlier and so Ella had been greeted by an empty house rather than the warm hug of her grandmother. Not quite knowing what to do, she had walked around the house until she had found the open basement window. She had climbed in and had been eating from Gram's full pantry and sleeping in the tiny sewing room ever since. From what I could gather, Ella had arrived only three or four days before I did.

She was finished and expecting my response. I was still reeling from the fact that Gus had a child he had never met. Serious and shy Uncle Gus. It just didn't seem possible. But Ella's eyes were all the proof I needed. There was no doubt that she had Uncle Gus's distinct, cobalt blue eyes. How had I not noticed how much she looks like him?

"Well, then, that means we are cousins!" I said, trying to inflect a happy tone into my voice in the midst of my bewilderment.

She gave me a tired, tentative smile.

"Well, there isn't much we can do about this situation tonight, so how about I tuck you into bed?"

I gave her a warm smile as I tried to remember something about little girls and bedtimes. The only thing I could recall is that Gram had always read to me. Was Ella too old to enjoy a story? It couldn't hurt to ask.

"Would you like me to read you a bedtime story? I am sure Gram has some storybooks around here somewhere," her eyes lit up at these words as she nodded her head.

An hour later, she was sound asleep, her blond hair fanned out against the pillow and a fisted hand next to her cheek.

I was completely unprepared for the maternal feelings that had welled up in me as I had helped my small, defenseless cousin prepare for bed. Snuggling together while reading to her from the red-covered book of Christmas stories had given me unexpected joy and pleasure. I had never even thought about children before. I had always been driven by my career. It was a foreign, but pleasant, feeling.

As soon as I walked into my bedroom, I realized that my bedding was still outside on the wash line. I sighed and turned to Buddy, "Come on, boy, we have one last thing to do before we can go to bed tonight."

Buddy wagged his tail and followed me.

"You know, it's been quite a day for you and me, hasn't it, boy? Lots of adventure. I can promise you that every day won't be like this one," I leaned down and petted his head as we walked out into the beautiful night together to pull the blankets from the line. Gram's light spring jacket that I had grabbed from the hook in the mud room wasn't keeping me very warm against the chill in the air, but I had to stop for just a moment to look at the stars, twinkling and shining in the black sky. You sure didn't see such a sight in the city. There were far too many man-made lights for that.

"What do you think, Buddy? Maybe this is where we are supposed to stay for good?"

I stood there praying for a few moments, asking the Lord to give me direction and wisdom, not only for my uncertain and murky future, but maybe even more importantly for the future of the sweet little girl that had literally been dropped in my lap.

"Please show me what to do," I whispered.

Grabbing the blankets, I headed inside.

The next morning, I was awakened by the little patter of feet. I lifted my head and saw Ella enter my room, carrying the Christmas storybook. Buddy lifted his head and wagged his tail against the comforter. (Against my better judgment, he had ended up on my bed last night. I just couldn't resist those big brown eyes!)

I had slept so much better than the night before but I wasn't quite ready to get out of bed so I patted the spot beside me and told her to climb up next to me.

She was soon snuggled in between Buddy and me, paging quietly through the book. I tried to close my eyes again, but the strangeness of having a little girl beside me kept me from sleep. In only a moment, I opened my eyes and sat up.

"Are you hungry?" I asked.

"Yes! Can you make pancakes?" She hopped out of bed with enthusiasm and started out the door, Buddy following close on her heels.

I followed after her, trying to reconcile this bright, talkative girl with the somber, quiet one from last night. She obviously had started to feel comfortable around me.

Suddenly, I realized that it was Christmas Eve. With everything going on, I had completely lost track of the days. I tried to think of a course of action for Ella. The first thing I knew I had to do was to find out if her mother was still alive, no matter what day it was.

I made some pancakes and we ate them amidst her happy chatter. After breakfast, I sent Ella up to get dressed. Meanwhile, I pulled out my laptop and tried to locate Melanie. Ella had told me that her last name was Erikson. Putting "Melanie Erikson" into the Google search box, I found a home address as well as a short article about a charity project she was part of at a Baptist church in her town.

I called the church, not really expecting an answer because of the holiday but was pleasantly surprised when the pastor picked up with a warm greeting. As I explained to him what had happened, he listened quietly and then told me that Melanie was in a local hospice facility and didn't have very long to live. And then he said sadly that when he had stopped by to visit Melanie yesterday, she was in terrible sorrow over not knowing if Ella was ok. She was heartbroken over not being able to say one final good-bye and was in utter despair over her rash decision to drop her daughter off at a stranger's house, even if it was her grandmother's. He was amazed that I was calling so shortly after he had had this conversation with her, as he had been praying just this morning about contacting Ella for Melanie.

I knew what I had to do. I thanked him for the information and turned to Ella, who was now dressed and quietly playing on the floor with Buddy.

The living room, with the twinkling tree lights and the cozy fire, set a nice atmosphere for us to talk about her mom. Ella, her arm around Buddy, listened intently as I explained that her mother was growing sicker every day but that she had changed her mind and really longed to say good-bye to her. Could she be brave and strong?

Ella's face grew pale but she sat up a little straighter and her eyes brightened at the prospect of seeing her mother, "When do we go? And what happens after that? Can I stay here with you?"

I had known that question was going to come eventually and I had thought of little else since I had found Ella the evening before. I had decided that if Ella wanted to stay with me, and if her mother was in agreement, I would offer her a home with me here at the farm house. This was a big part of my reason for finding Melanie. I knew that Ella would be thrown into the state foster system if I couldn't get some kind of signed, legal document from her mother.

"Ella, would you like to stay here and live with me at the farm house?"

"Oh, yes! Please!" Only three little words, but the passion in her little heart glistened through her amazing blue eyes.

"Okay, then, let's see if we can make that happen," I smiled at her as the ramifications of what I had just said filled my head. Instant motherhood. Was I really ready for this? But I knew I had to take care of this dear little cousin of mine. She had no one else in the world. And then it dawned on me—neither did I. We were perfectly suited for one another.

I put Buddy in his crate and we started out. Ella was mostly quiet on the drive, probably thinking about her mother. In a little over an hour, we were pulling into the parking lot that stood in front of a pretty stone building with wreaths in the windows.

A kind lady directed us to Melanie's room and we were soon at her door. I took a deep breath and knocked.

"Melanie? Are you feeling well enough for visitors?" I hesitantly pushed the door open.

I am not sure what I was expecting but it wasn't this shell of a woman who looked like she weighed less than 90 pounds.

I could see the question in her eyes and then she saw Ella. Her eyes, dull and lifeless a second before, noticeably brightened.

"Ella? Is that my baby? Am I dreaming?"

Ella walked over to her mom and leaned over to gently kiss her.

"No, Melanie, you aren't dreaming. Ella is here to say good-bye."

"Oh, my baby, my baby," Melanie moaned, "I can't believe you are here. I didn't want you to see me like this, but I am so glad you are here."

I quietly moved back to a dark corner of the room to let them have a few moments alone.

They talked in low tones for a while and then I heard Melanie, with a desperate note in her voice, ask, "Ella, are you okay?"

"Yes, mom, I am fine. Libby is taking good care of me." I was so glad that she didn't expand on all she had been through.

"Who is Libby? Where is your grandmother?" The question was expected and I stepped up to explain.

"Melanie, I am Libby," I introduced myself and then continued, "I am Ella's cousin. Gus was my mom's little brother and my uncle. Our grandmother died a few months ago and, of course, you didn't know that. But please don't worry, I have been caring for Ella. I would be happy to continue caring for her if that would that be okay with you?"

I recognized even as I spoke what a vulnerable place Melanie was in. She didn't know me at all. She didn't know if I was telling the truth. She was literally putting her daughter in the hands of a stranger. And she didn't have the strength or the resources to even check my story.

With this in mind, I pulled out some of the most recent photos I had with Uncle Gus. There weren't many but I had found a few in Grandma's old photo albums. There was the one where we stood together on the porch a few summers ago, drinking tall glasses of iced tea. And then there was the one where we stood smiling down at the camera from the roof where we were putting up Christmas lights. Showing her these and a few others seemed to erase some of the worry lines from her forehead.

I gently held Melanie's hand and looked her in the eye.

"Melanie, I promise to love Ella as my own. I know you don't know me but I want to assure you that you can trust me. I will care for her."

I saw two tears make a path down Melanie's cheek and then she breathed out words I wasn't expecting.

"I have regretted my decision to drop off Ella every minute since I left her. I knew her grandmother would take care of her–I had no doubts about that—but I should have stayed. I should have asked. I wasn't thinking. I was scared. I couldn't think beyond the pain and desperation."

"It's okay. You don't have to explain," I could see how difficult this was for her, both physically and emotionally. Every word seemed laborious. But she continued.

"Please...let me finish," she weakly pleaded and then continued, "as I approach the end, I mostly sleep..." she stopped and took a shallow breath, "but any moment I am awake, I have prayed, begging the Lord to assure me that my baby will be okay," another pause and then, finally, "You are the answer to that prayer. I am sure of it," she smiled then and added, "Gus used to talk about you so fondly. He really loved you, you know. I believe that God has sent you here with Ella as an answer to my prayer. And I am so grateful."

Right at that moment, I was in awe over God's sovereign plan for all of us. I knew God would work out every detail somehow. But I also knew that I had something that had to be done.

"Melanie, do you feel well enough to sign a letter that would give me custody of Ella?"

"Yes, yes, of course, it must be done," she struggled to sit up.

"No, no, not yet. I am going to go call a friend of mine. Ella will stay here with you and visit. I'll be back."

I went out to the nurses' station and asked for paper and a pen and then lost no time in calling Kate. Mrs. Miller had said that Kate was in grad school, but Kate told me yesterday that she was actually in law school. She had laughingly said her grandma could never remember that. I knew she could help me.

Soon I had a letter drafted that would hopefully hold up in court. Melanie gladly signed it as two nurses stood by and then signed as witnesses.

And then it was just the three of us alone in that dark, somber room. With tears streaming down her face, Melanie said her final good-bye to Ella. I offered to bring Ella back for another visit but she lifted a weak hand in protest and said, "I won't be here much longer now. I'm going home soon."

As we prepared to leave, she reached for my hand and said the words I will never forget: "Thank you, Libby, for taking care of my little girl. Please teach her to love Jesus with all of her heart."

Her hand dropped and, exhausted, she closed her eyes. I could see she was spent. We probably had stayed too long. We were all crying but Ella was sobbing almost uncontrollably. I put my arm around her as we slowly walked away. I am not sure I have ever done anything so hard as leave that room.

I asked a nurse to check on Melanie as we left, letting them know that she may be upset. The nurse smiled and told us that we were the best medicine she could have ever had. Apparently, the nursing staff knew her story and had been praying, as well, for a miracle. One nurse had even started a search for Ella and had planned a trip to our town tomorrow in order to find her. It was pretty amazing to be part of such a marvelous answer to prayer.

A few hours later, Ella and I were sitting alongside the Millers in a church pew. I think we both were overwhelmed at the changes in our lives over the past few days. There was so much to take in.

Both mourning and joy were part of what we were feeling. All that we had lost was competing with the newfound joy of having found each other. What a Christmas!

As the congregation started to sing *Joy to the World*, I grabbed Ella's hand and squeezed it. She looked at me with a bright smile and I knew that, eventually, we would both be okay.

We had both found a family this Christmas. An unexpected little family that we both had needed so desperately. God had taken such special care of both of us and I knew He would continue to do so. I moved my thoughts back to the service and joined the singing with gusto. *Joy to the world, the Lord is Come!*

Mending Fences

I don't know when it happened but one day, I realized that I couldn't remember what she looked like. Not that it mattered. She probably had changed, anyway. And it wasn't like I was going to see her anytime soon. But it still filled me with sorrow that I couldn't remember her face.

I sat on my front porch, deep in reflection. The smell of autumn was in the air and a cool wind had forced me to don a light sweater. This time of year always made me nostalgic. It brought memories of school days, football games, and the much-anticipated preparation for the holiday season at Dad's store.

My thoughts turned back to my sister. I squinted my eyes as I tried to picture her in my mind. I remembered that she had straight brown hair. And greenish eyes hidden by glasses that seemed to only enhance her beauty rather than detract from it. But the rest just seemed to be lost in the vague recesses of my memory. How could I have forgotten what my sister looks like? The thought startled and scared me at the same time. A part of my past was escaping my memory and it deeply saddened me.

I went back into the house and climbed the stairs to the attic. I turned on the light and started making my way through the collection of boxes kept there. There was a photo album from my past somewhere in all of those relics. I finally spotted the gray container that held all my old albums. I found the frayed, green photo album I was looking for as soon as I opened the bin.

I sat down on a sturdy box nearby and started paging through it. Ahh, there she was. My beautiful, green-eyed sister with the tortoise shell glasses and thick brown hair that fell just a little below her shoulders. The perfect nose and high cheek bones gave her a special type of beauty that I had not inherited.

I wondered if she still wore her hair like this? Did she still wear glasses or did she have contacts now? It had been fifteen years since we had laid eyes on each other. Could it have really been that long?

It was with great regret that I remembered that we hadn't even talked to each other that last time. The awkwardness of Daddy's funeral came back in a rush. The great efforts we both made to try and avoid one another. The rapid heartbeat and dropped eyes when she drew near. The lack of desire to even speak to her. Her lack of interest in Greta, her only niece. I could remember it all like it was yesterday.

But one does a lot of growing up in fifteen years. And now I found myself wishing I had done a lot of things differently. *If onlys* plagued me.

If I had to do over, I would change things. I really would. But I recognized the futility of that thought.

"Mom?" Greta stirred me out of my reverie.

"Up here, honey! I'll be right down!"

Sighing, I placed the photo album back into the box and placed the lid on top. A few hours later, our Friday pizza and movie night was over and Greta was sleeping soundly in her room. As I sat on the sofa in the family room, my mind went back to the past.

Life has a way of stealing our happy endings. And so it was with me. But maybe I had short-changed myself. I was simply reaping what I had sown.

Perhaps I should start at the beginning. That would help all of this make more sense to you.

Once upon a time (don't all stories begin this way?) there were two sisters. Evie, the firstborn, was shy and quiet. Her younger sister, Eliza, was boisterous and outgoing. But the two were inseparable from the very beginning.

Doesn't that sound nice? Just like a lovely story you might read in an actual book.

Except that the lovely story ended up not so lovely. I'm Eliza. The younger sister by only 15 months. And Evie and I were best friends. Together we navigated playgrounds, middle school, and teen-aged angst. Together we weathered broken friendships, boyfriend break-ups, and frustrations with Mom and Dad.

Memories started flooding my mind as I recalled those days. Like the time when Marcy, my best school friend of several years, just decided one day that she liked Lauren better than she liked me. From that time on, I watched the two girls eat lunch side-by-side, climb the monkey bars at recess, and sit beside each other at every opportunity—all while I sat alone and uninvited to their circle. Oh, how I had cried. It was Evie who comforted me. Evie who wrapped her small arms around me so tightly and said, "now, don't you worry! We are sisters and sisters are best friends for life! Who needs them, anyway?"

I felt my eyes start to burn. Oh, the turns that life takes. I wondered what would have happened if Rick had never set foot in dad's store? How would our lives have been different?

As I sat on the sofa, my mind went back to that first time I saw Rick. Evie's best friend, Monica, had introduced her to Rick at a football game and it didn't take them long to become inseparable. After just a few weeks she asked if she could bring him around for dinner. Mom had prepared her delicious roast beef and made-from-scratch mashed potatoes in Rick's honor. For dessert, she had made a chocolate cake with a thick frosting of peanut butter icing. Isn't it funny what you remember about certain moments?

Evie was 23 and had just settled into a good accounting job upon her graduation from the local university the preceding May. And she was ready to get married. It didn't take her more than a few weeks of dating to believe that Rick was her future husband.

I was 21 and working at Dad's store while I tried to figure out what I wanted to do with my life. Dad and I got along well and it seemed like the perfect fit for the time being.

Our whole family loved Rick from the very beginning. He was laid back and funny and had twinkling light blue eyes that lit up when he talked to you. By the end of the evening, my dad had offered him a job at the store and I...well...I had fallen hopelessly in love.

For the next year, I put on a pretty good act. No one knew I was head over heels in love with my sister's handsome boyfriend. Well, Mom might have figured it out but if she did, she didn't say anything.

But working together at the store had given us a special, albeit platonic, relationship. We had a lot of fun together. He teased me and I teased back. I think he enjoyed my lightheartedness and love for fun in comparison to my very serious-minded sister.

One day, my sister came home with a ring on her finger. How it is possible to be so happy and so heartbroken at the same time is truly a mystery, but as both emotions washed over me, I told myself that I must move on. Rick was Evie's. He would never be mine. I must resign myself to that.

Mom had caught my eye as I hugged Evie tightly and wished her the best. It was then that I realized that she most certainly did realize how I felt about Rick. I gave her a wry smile and went to my room.

A little later she came to talk to me. She told me she knew this was hard for me, but that I must be more careful with Rick now that he was engaged. She realized he treated me like a little sister, but I must be careful not to show my true feelings. For Evie's sake and for Rick's, too.

I told Mom I understood and she left. And I really did understand. Of course, I didn't plan for anything to happen between Rick and me. What loving sister and best friend ever would? I knew what was right.

But, of course, one rarely does plan for these types of things.

One night, a few weeks after my conversation with Mom, I found myself in an undesirable situation. Christmas was always a busy time but this particular year it was extra busy because Dad was opening a second store in a nearby town. This demanded a lot of Dad's time and so I was left to run the store many times on my own. Thankfully, it was always with one of the local high school kids that helped us out, as Dad had Rick at the new store more often than not. I found this a huge relief and honestly believed that my feelings were waning and I was ready to move on with life.

But then, just a week before Christmas, came that one unexpected and dreaded night. Dad, completely unaware of my feelings, left Rick and me alone at the store.

As we were closing for the night, we ended up in the back store room together. I had tried so hard to avoid this moment, always being so careful to not be alone with my sister's fiancé. But when the moment finally presented itself, I caved. I am ashamed to admit it, but all of those feelings hid deep inside rushed to the surface and I caved.

I am pretty sure Rick didn't mean for it to happen, either. Although I have always wondered about that. I guess I'll never know.

My face grew hot as I remembered the rest of that night. What had I been thinking? My parents were very moral people. We didn't go to church but I was raised right. I definitely knew the difference between right and wrong and that this was so wrong. How in the world could I have sacrificed the friendship of my sister and destroyed my family for a few stolen moments? I realized the sheer stupidity and blatant immorality of it all immediately afterwards.

But it was too late. Within a year, life had utterly and completely changed forever: Evie had sworn she would never forgive me and moved away to California. Rick disappeared from the scene altogether and none of us ever saw him again. And I was a single mom to a baby girl who looked an awful lot like Rick. I named her Greta.

"Good morning, Mom! Didn't you ever go to bed?" Greta said brightly, waking me up with her words.

I groggily looked around me and realized that I was still on the sofa where I had relived those awful years over again in my mind the night before. I smiled at that baby girl, who was now so grown up.

"Good morning, sweetheart. What's on your schedule today?"

"I have two classes and then I will be at work for the dinner shift. I'll just study at the library in between classes today." Greta was in her second year at the community college nearby and also worked at the local diner.

"Hope you have a wonderful day!" I gave her a big hug as I raised myself out of the comfortable corner of the couch that had been my bed the night before.

"You, too, Mom. What are you doing today?"

"That's a good question," I laughed. I had off work today and I was still thinking through what I wanted to get done.

Greta headed out the door and I walked to the kitchen to make a cup of coffee. Still in my clothing from last night and looking quite rumpled, I looked rather like a vagabond.

After breakfast and a shower, I decided I'd go see Mom. She lived in an assisted living community nearby. She had never really recovered after Dad died 15 years ago. Never being that strong to begin with, his sudden death from a heart attack had left her heartbroken and in a weakened physical state. About eight years ago now, I had arranged for her to go to Good Shepherd Assisted Living.

It was around that same time that I started attending Trinity Bible Church, located a couple of blocks from where we lived. I am not sure what drove me to go to church on that particular Sunday but I knew I needed something to help me with the horrible guilt I had lived with since that fateful night was like a million pound rock on my back.

It was through Pastor Jack and his wife, Patty, that I found out about God's forgiveness. They opened the Bible and showed me from its pages how Jesus had died for me and that no matter what sin I had committed, forgiveness was available for me.

It had taken me several months to actually believe that I could be forgiven for something so awful. But when I finally repented and surrendered my life to Jesus, that million-pound rock had rolled right off my shoulders! I hadn't even realized how heavy it was until it was gone.

Greta was saved just a few months after I was and then Mom shortly after that. All three of us had been going to TBC ever since and, within a year, that small church on the corner was like the extended family we never had. It was there that we grew in our faith through the expository preaching of the Word and the discipleship of those who were more mature in the faith. I thanked God most every day for His kindness in leading me to that truth-teaching church and showing me the way to salvation.

Since coming to know the Lord, the one thing that had really been on my mind was my sister. A few years after I was saved, I read Romans and came across this small, powerful verse towards the end of chapter 12: *If it is possible, as much as depends on you, live peaceably with all men.*

I found myself wondering if I had done everything possible to be at peace with my sister?

This time of year was especially hard. October was when we'd have so much fun preparing for the holidays in Dad's store. Every year I thought about reaching out to her and every year I chickened out. I just knew she would reject me again and I wasn't sure I could bear it.

California had treated her well. She had a great job and had ended up marrying a guy named Steve. They were busily raising their children. I only knew this because she communicated occasionally with Mom. But poor Mom had never even met her grandkids. Their happy faces were in frames on the wall of her small apartment but she had never heard their voices or put her arms around them.

I felt responsible for this, too. Evie was still so angry with me that she hadn't even brought her kids to meet their grandma. Oh, the burden was so hard to bear. The Lord, in His awesome grace and mercy, had taken away the guilt and the shame, but I still lived with the pain and the devastating consequences. They would always be with me, I imagined.

The only good to come from that awful time was Greta. Oh, how I thanked the Lord for my precious daughter. She was the one and only bright spot in the whole affair.

What if you would just try just one last time to reach out to Evie?

The thought came unbidden and totally unexpectedly. Could I risk it? But what was I even risking? She couldn't reject me any more than she already had. Surely, it would be worth at least trying—if not just for Mom's sake.

Yes. I would try.

"But it won't work," the little voice in my mind insisted.

The memory of the last time I had tried to apologize came rushing back. It was shortly before Dad had died. I had called her for the third and final time in my efforts to make things right. But before I could even get one sentence out, she had firmly said in a stone-cold voice that she would never, ever forgive me and to never call her again.

I never had.

But that was over fifteen years ago now. Since that time, she had gotten married and had three kids. Would she see things a little differently now? Since Bryce had been born, she called Mom a lot more often. Maybe she was changing, too. Like I was.

I decided to sit down and write her a letter before I lost my courage. I called Mom and told her I'd be a little later than I had planned and then sat down to write. I read and re-read the letter. I erased and re-wrote.

I crumpled the first and then the second and third drafts in my hand and threw them in the trash. But finally, I had penned this letter—

Dear Evie—

I have been wanting to write this letter for such a long time now. Nineteen years ago I sinned against you in a way that is truly unforgivable.

I cannot begin to tell you how many times I have wished that I could go back and change what happened. But, to my great sorrow, I can't. I can't fix it. I can't change it. I can't undo it.

But I want to ask you just one last time to forgive me. I beg you to forgive me for betraying you. I sinned against you in one of the worst ways possible and I have regretted it every single day since. But I love you, Evie. I always have and I always will. It would be my greatest desire to restore our relationship.

Your Sister, Eliza

I sucked in my breath as the tears rolled down my face. One of them dropped on the letter, smearing the *E* in my name. Should I write it again?

I sighed and realized that I didn't have the emotional energy to write it again. I shrugged my shoulders and folded up the letter. I stuck it in an envelope and then popped it into my purse. I needed to get her current address from Mom.

I didn't even have my sister's address, I realized, my heart sinking. Oh, what a sad and sorry state of affairs. But with God's help, perhaps we could start rebuilding this family. And maybe it would start with my letter. The tiniest bit of hope started beating in my breast.

The phone rang and I anxiously looked at the caller ID, praying I'd see my sister's name. It had been five weeks since I had sent the letter and hope still surged in me every time I heard the phone ring. But I hadn't received a phone call, a letter, or an email with any indication that she had even gotten the letter. In fact, it was like I hadn't even sent it.

I answered the call and took care of a minor situation at work. It was my day off again and I had arranged to pick up Mom and meet Greta for lunch close to her school. It was almost Christmas now and holiday decorations and lights were everywhere. I loved this time of year!

I climbed in to my Honda Accord and put on some Bing Crosby for Mom. She just loved listening to the tunes from her past. Especially during the holiday season. I think they reminded her of better days.

In an hour, Mom was in my car and we were driving as sporadic snowflakes fell around the car. The weatherman was calling for a couple of inches of snow later on in the day. I glanced up at the leaden sky, hoping it would hold off until we were all home safe.

Greta was waiting for us at the restaurant. I held on to Mom's arm as I led her over to the booth.

"Hi, Mom! Hi, Grandma!" Greta gave her a warm hug.

"Oh, hello, dear! How are you doing?" Mom's face always lit up in Greta's presence.

After ordering hamburgers and fries, we started talking about the holidays while we sipped on our cokes. It had been just the three of us since Dad had died and we chatted about our normal Christmas traditions. Greta suggested we start some new ones

"I think we should build a gingerbread house. How about it, Gram? You want to help?"

"Sure, dear. I'll do what I can. I used to make some pretty good gingerbread in my day. I wonder if I can remember how?" Mom's brow crinkled as she tried to remember her recipe.

As she and Greta talked about gingerbread, I thought of all of the heartache I had caused her and almost started to cry. Ever since I had sent that letter I seemed to be more emotional. I just wished Evie would answer one way or another. But that tiny bit of hope that had risen inside me when I sent the letter was starting to dwindle now.

"Mom, are you okay?" Greta knew me so well.

"Sure," I gave a wry smile.

"Gram, Mom just hasn't been herself recently. Do you know what's going on?" Greta addressed the words to her grandmother but her pale blue eyes were questioning me.

"I do not, but I most certainly agree with you. I have been thinking the same thing. What is wrong, Eliza? You haven't been yourself for weeks now," Mom's direct question made me squirm. Why couldn't I be a better actress? I really did not want to have this discussion.

"I'm okay—" I started.

With those words, my mom grabbed my hands and her green eyes—so like Evie's—grew very serious as she looked straight at me, "Honey, it's alright to say you'd rather not say but it is not okay to lie."

I looked at her. And then at Greta. And then I sighed as one small tear made its way down the right side of my face.

"Mom, what's going on?"

"Alright. I'll just tell you. I decided to send Evie a letter, asking her one last time to forgive me. I had so hoped our restored relationship might be my best ever Christmas gift to you, Mom. But that was five weeks ago now and she hasn't even bothered to respond. I guess I just need to realize that our relationship will never be healed. It is what it is. But it's hard."

Mom sighed and then said these wise words: "You know something I have learned through the years? Forgiveness is a two-way street. You can't force someone to forgive you. You did the right thing and I'm proud of you. The ball is in Evie's court now. Why don't we pray for her right now?"

And so we lifted Evie up to the Lord right there in the restaurant booth, begging God to help her to forgive me. Asking Him to soften her heart so that we could tell her all about Jesus and what He had done for us. And for her, too.

I hummed merrily along with the Christmas music playing on the TV. The music, along with the fake crackling fireplace picture, was courtesy of a local TV station. It would play for a few hours on this Christmas morning.

I gathered the ingredients for my homemade apple spice coffee cake and started mixing it up. It was a long-time tradition and one we all loved. I'd put it in the oven and then go and get Mom and bring her here for the day.

Greta came sleepily into the kitchen while I was making it.

"Merry Christmas!" I said cheerily.

"Merry Christmas," she groaned, "why is it that the older you get the less you care about getting up on Christmas morning?"

"That just means you are growing up!" I laughed. We chatted light-heartedly for a few moments and then her face grew serious.

"So Aunt Evie never contacted you?" she asked. It had been two weeks since we had prayed in that booth.

And the three of us had continued to pray—sometimes together and sometimes alone— every day since then.

The world that had seemed bright and cheery only a moment before suddenly darkened.

"No, she didn't. I guess it will never happen. But God has His reasons. I can't change her. I can only control me."

And I realized that this is what I had learned through the whole ordeal. While I was deeply saddened that Evie wouldn't forgive me, I recognized that I had now done all I could do and, in that, I found peace. I had lived out Romans 12:18 and it had changed my perspective.

While peace with God was always possible through His Son, peace with and between people was not always possible. I needed to learn to be okay with this hard truth. I think I finally understood that now.

"Well, we will have a great Christmas, anyway!" I grabbed my jacket and blew Greta a kiss, "I'm going to go get Gram. Can you take the cake out when the timer goes off? I might be back because it needs to bake a full hour, but just in case—"

"Sure, Mom. I'm going to go read but I promise that I will listen for the timer. See you soon," Greta smiled as she waved with a Jane Austen novel in her hand. She poured herself a glass of orange juice and took it, along with her book, to her favorite chair in the family room.

It took me considerably less than an hour to pick up Mom. Traffic was light on this Christmas morning and I was soon pulling into my driveway.

In front of the house was an unfamiliar silver SUV. For a brief moment I wondered who was visiting, but then I remembered that the neighbors often had their visitors park in front of our house. They must have some family visiting for Christmas.

I went around to the passenger side of my car so that I could help Mom walk across the icy driveway. It had snowed lightly again last night and with the cold temperatures it just wasn't melting. She gave me a hard time for helping her but I knew, deep down, she appreciated it.

I opened the front door to the sound of voices. At first, I thought it was just the TV but then I recognized one voice.

No...

It couldn't possibly be...

"Evie?!" Mom shouted her name with glee. She pulled away from me and Mom and daughter ran toward each other.

"Evie! Oh, Evie! I knew you'd come! I just knew you would!"

Tears streamed down both of their faces. I, on the other hand, stood back. I was still unsure exactly how this would go. It had been a very long time and there was so very much "water under the bridge".

After a few minutes, Evie pulled herself from Mom's embrace and turned toward me.

"I have decided that enough is enough. I want to forgive you. I am working on it. This is my first step towards forgiveness." She said hesitantly and then proceeded to introduce us to her family.

Her husband, Steve, stepped forward and shook my hand. His thick, wavy blonde hair and glasses, his firm handshake, and his serious gray eyes were nothing like Rick's. I was thankful for this. And then she pulled her children forward. Ten-year old Bryce looked just like his father. Eight-year-old Trace looked like Evie. And five-year old Savannah looked like...

"Why she is the spitting image of you, Eliza!" My mom said what we were all thinking.

"She is, isn't she?" My sister laughed and it was a happy laugh. It was the laugh I remembered from our childhood days.

And that's the exact moment that I knew that everything was going to be alright.

And it was. From that time forward, the two sisters became friends again. Eventually they became best friends again. But that would take some time.

For this year, it was enough for me that we were together. It was the best Christmas gift ever!

The Christmas Ornaments

Julie sighed. Pulling her frayed sweater around her shoulders, she trudged on through the slush. Sleet fell hard on her shoulders as she walked down the street to her tiny apartment on the upper floor of an old historical brownstone. Adding a bright note to the dreary night were twinkling Christmas trees in the windows and Christmas lights strung from porch roofs and wrapped around lamp posts.

Biting her lip with worry, she wondered how she would pay the rent this month. Things were so tight. Waitressing just wasn't providing her enough to live on. Especially now that they had cut her hours back. She thought of poor Mrs. Gunderson who had lost her husband a year ago. The restaurant was sorely missing its owner and manager. The owner's wife seemed to be doing all she could, but it just wasn't working. Mr. Gunderson had been the face of the Diner. He had been the reason for his establishment's success. His fun, lively spirit and excellent management, along with a caring heart had made him one of the town's favorite people. Some people you just couldn't replace.

Julie knew she should get another job and yet thinking about leaving Mrs. Gunderson in this difficult time just seemed cruel. She sighed again as her options—or lack thereof—trailed through her mind.

"I'm too tired to think about it tonight," she thought as she climbed the porch steps of her apartment building. Entering the huge foyer that served as an entry way, she stopped to check her mail and found an unexpected surprise: A small nondescript, brown package with her name and address written in a Christmassy red and green.

Curious, she put it, along with the bills and flyers in her box, in her tote bag and went up the stairs to her apartment. Putting the key in the old wooden door, she heard it creak just a bit as she opened it.

Oh, it was so chilly! She turned up the heat by a degree or two, trying not to think about the extra expense. Mr. Tibbs, her orange cat, rubbed against her legs.

"Hello there, Mr. Tibbs. How was your day?" Julie reached down and picked the cat up, cuddling him in her arms. She didn't really consider herself a cat person, but Mr. Tibbs had shown up in the yard downstairs one day and no one wanted him. After some effort to find his owner, Julie had eventually claimed him, growing quite attached during the process.

But there were matters more pressing than cuddling Mr. Tibbs and she put him back down and took the mysterious package over to the table. A scissors quickly opened the box and there, in a soft bed of bubble wrap, lay a miniature snow globe. A ribbon was attached, indicating that it was a Christmas ornament. She shook it up and down and watched the snow fall on the tiny Christ child who lay in a miniature manger with His parents close by.

She reached her hand into the package to look for a card. Finding an envelope, she pulled it out and opened it. Her eyes widened in great surprise at the wad of bills inside. *What in the world?* She wondered.

She counted them and found ten one hundred dollar bills along with a small post-it note that said only these simple words: *Merry Christmas! I'm praying for you!*

Julie thought through all of the people she knew and realized she didn't know even one person who could afford to send this kind of cash. Who could it be?

The next day she awoke to the pleasant realization that her rent was no longer a problem. The gift she had received yesterday would more than cover it. In fact, she could put several hundred away and still have a bit to spend on Christmas. She couldn't remember the last time she had even a dollar that could be spent frivolously. She didn't go to work until the dinner shift that evening and so she decided she would go have some fun. She hadn't planned on getting a tree but now that she had this little ornament, perhaps a small tree was in order.

The crisp, bright weather outside seemed to echo her mood. The sun shone brightly from the blue sky as she walked into the city to do a little shopping.

Beginning at her favorite department store, she found a small artificial tree for her ornament. She bought a few other ornaments and some mini-lights to complete the tree. Her heart welled up with excitement at the thought of decorating it. It had been so long since she had even celebrated Christmas. She hadn't realized how much she missed it until she received the ornament.

Next, she went to the pet department, where she purchased a cloth mouse that squeaked and two little tinkling balls in bright colors for Mr. Tibbs.

The women's clothing department was next on her list and there she picked out a new soft and thick heather gray sweater. She even found a much-needed winter coat on sale. It was a bright pink color—most likely the reason it was on clearance—but she bought it anyway. It was so much warmer than the thin, worn out coat she had had since she was a teenager.

Within a couple of hours she had made her purchases and was struggling to carry them home. She should have thought about that, she berated herself. The bag with the ornaments kept falling.

"Here let me help you with that," A young man jumped to her aid just as the bag was getting ready to slip again.

"Oh, thank you so much!" She laughed as she accepted his help. She noticed his warm brown eyes.

"Where are you headed?" He asked in a friendly manner.

When she told him her street, he whistled, "That's a long way with a load this heavy. Why don't I flag a taxi for you?"

"Oh, no, I'll be fine—" and then she remembered. Just this once, she could afford a taxi. She thanked him for his kindness and waited on the sidewalk as he held his hand out.

Within a few moments, she was cozily settled into the taxi with all of her packages.

"Thank you!" she said to the nice man but he had already turned and was walking away.

A few hours later, she was at work. But, unlike the previous days, there was a spring in her step and she hurried to the booth where her favorite customer, Mrs. Bailey, sat.

"Good evening, Mrs. Bailey!"

"Good evening, dear. So nice to see you."

"Where is Mr. Bailey tonight? Still under the weather?"

"He still has that cold. He just can't seem to shake that awful cough. His nurse seems worried. I left him in her care and thought I'd come out for a quick bite to eat."

In the four years that Julie had worked at the restaurant, Mrs. Bailey had been joined by Mr. Bailey faithfully until the past three months. He had caught a terrible case of bronchitis and his 83-year-old body was having a very hard time recovering.

The Baileys had never had kids and had expressed how lonely they were. In this, Julie had felt a kinship with them and they had developed a relationship that went beyond just a few meals at the restaurant.

"Please let him know I asked after him."

"I will surely do that, dear. You should come and visit when you can. I know that would cheer him up."

The Bailey's lived in a tiny apartment in a nice neighborhood just a short walk from the restaurant. Julie had been there often.

"Yes, I will have to do that," she smiled, "now what can I get you?"

A few moments later she carried out a steaming bowl of creamy potato soup along with a cup of coffee for her friend. Behind her, at a nearby table, someone sat watching.

"Well, that looks delicious. I think I'll have the same," said a slightly familiar voice.

Julie turned and, surprised, saw that it was the friendly man from earlier that day. He sat with a pretty blonde woman.

They were sitting in her section and so, smiling, Julie walked over to the table with her pad in hand, ready to take their order.

The man gave a big grin and said, "Well, if it isn't the girl with too many packages from earlier today! What are the chances?"

He introduced her to his pretty wife, who was as friendly as he was. It was a slow evening at the restaurant and this gave her an opportunity to talk with the young couple. She found out their names were Ted and Maggie. Before they left, they extended an invitation to come to the young people's meetings at their church. When they explained where it was, Julie realized that Grace Bible Church was not too far from her house and decided she would go. She was ready to try something new.

The following December found Julie at a much different place. Oh, she was still in the old brownstone struggling to make ends meet, but life had sure changed in other ways. It had all begun with the tiny snow globe from the anonymous sender. As Julie pulled it out of its careful wrapping, she reflected on this.

A couple of weeks after she had met Ted and Maggie at the restaurant, she had been true to her word and she had gone to their church. They had greeted her kindly and invited her to sit with them.

Their genuine kindness had met a need deep inside her. But the pastor's message met a spiritual need that she didn't even know she had. As she had listened to the pastor speak about sin and how no human can do anything to merit salvation on their own, she grew slightly uncomfortable. This was unlike any other message she had ever heard.

She thought back to her own childhood, where she attended a church that taught that the only way to be saved was to be morally good. And, while she did try to be a good person, she grew tired of the hopelessness and eternal striving to be perfect. She walked away from that church and never looked back.

But now here was this preacher telling her that salvation and reaching heaven wasn't even about good works. This lit a fire in Julie's heart and the Lord was surely drawing her to Himself.

She went home and started reading her Bible—something she had never done before. She asked questions to Ted and Maggie, who patiently answered and never made her feel foolish.

Within a few months, she had come to understand that she was a sinner and that Christ alone was her salvation. He had died for her sins and covered them with His blood. A newfound peace filled her heart and a deep love for her Savior grew.

Over the course of that winter, Ted and Maggie "adopted" Julie into their family. She became Aunt Julie to their two girls, three-year-old Lucy and one-year-old Ava. She started spending each Tuesday evening with them, eating and talking and helping with the girls. As Julie's only remaining family was distant and far-flung, she grew to consider them as her family.

When springtime arrived, it was with a newfound enthusiasm for life. With a spring in her step and a brighter smile on her face, she had served the customers at Gunderson's Diner. Suddenly her life, which had seemed so hopeless a few months before, was full of hope and joy.

Of course, her money troubles didn't go away just because she was now saved and, sometime in the summer, she started thinking about changing jobs. Mrs. Gunderson had started talking about selling the diner and Julie finally felt like she could leave. But to where? To do what?

She thought about the money she had tucked away in savings last Christmas. Quite suddenly, a thought came to her: Perhaps she could start taking classes? The thought grew like a flower within her and soon it had fully blossomed. Yes! That is exactly what she would do.

She had poured over the catalog of the local community college and finally settled on nursing.

Perhaps she could get her degree in nursing, one class at a time. She met with an advisor and was soon scheduled for two classes during the fall semester—both paid for by the generous Christmas benefactor.

Sometime in October, Jack had entered her life. Thinking of Jack made Julie pause in her reflection temporarily as she glanced down at her watch. He was picking her up for a Christmas concert in a few minutes and she wanted to be ready. The watch indicated she had ten more minutes, so she let her mind wander back to when she first met him.

Jack was the younger brother of Ted. He had grown tired of city life and longed to be closer to his family. And so he had found a job in their town, packed his bags, and moved into a condo a short distance from Ted and Maggie's neighborhood.

With Jack came fun and laughter and yet he had a serious side, too. When Ted and Maggie had introduced them, they quickly realized they were kindred spirits. They became good friends immediately and, within a few weeks, they started dating.

Julie lingered on her thoughts of Jack. She never dreamed that she would meet someone like him. He was kind and generous and, most important of all, he loved the Lord. God had been so good to bring Jack into her life. It was hard to imagine life without him already, although it had only been two short months.

Suddenly, she heard a knock at her door. She opened it to Jack's smiling face.

"Look what I found in your mailbox," he enthusiastically tossed a package to her. Julie had enjoyed a long, lazy Saturday in her apartment decorating for Christmas and had asked Jack to get her mail on his way up.

"This looks very similar to the one from last year," she mused as she began to open it.

A few moments later she was pulling out a beautiful hand-made wooden cross ornament along with a thick wad of cash.

Jack's eyes widened as he whistled long and low, "well, look at that."

Julie carefully hung the beautiful little cross on her tree and then counted out exactly one thousand dollars. A little note accompanied it: *Merry Christmas! I continue to pray for you.*

After the concert, as Jack and Julie lingered over coffee, they talked about who could have sent the package. Not just once—but two years in a row. But not even one of their ideas seemed plausible.

"Maybe it's a rich relative," Jack surmised.

Julie furled her brow. She remembered that she did have a wealthy great-great aunt in Boston. And she thought there might be a couple of great uncles down south somewhere. She couldn't imagine them sending her money or, even more strangely, praying for a girl they hadn't seen since she was three or four. But she supposed stranger things had happened.

Julie discussed it with Ted and Maggie, Mrs. Gunderson, her boss, and Mrs. Bailey, her favorite customer. They all offered helpful suggestions but to no avail. The sender remained a mystery.

A year later, Jack and Julie were engaged and excitedly planning their June wedding. It would be a small affair, with the majority of the wedding guests from their church family. Jack's family would make up the rest of the guest list. Julie was an only child and had lost her parents in a car accident a few years ago. She would invite what little family she had left but she doubted they would come such a long way.

The two worked extra hours to help pay for the wedding. Thankfully, Jack's parents had generously offered to pay for their wedding reception and so that was a big weight off of their minds.

As Christmas approached, Julie had started thinking about what wedding expenses she could cover with the $1000 gift she hoped to receive again.

She'd try to remind herself that there was no guarantee the ornament, along with the generous gift of money, would show up again this year. But then her mind would take off again and she'd be dreamily thinking of what special thing could be purchased.

However, as the weeks passed by, she had to start considering the fact that it might not be coming this year.

Julie continued to take nursing classes, where she was doing very well. She also continued to work at the restaurant where Mr. and Mrs. Gunderson's son, John, had surprisingly stepped up to be its manager. It seemed that he couldn't bear to see the diner leave the family's hands and so he had left his well-paying management job and had moved his family from Dallas, TX, back to his hometown in the east.

Julie found John to be a friendly and astute man in his mid-forties. He had brought back the stability that had disappeared upon his father's death and things had steadily improved at the restaurant. Mrs. Gunderson still helped out but she was so much less stressed now that John was in control.

Sadly, Mr. Bailey had passed away in March from complications of pneumonia. Mrs. Bailey became even more regular at the diner now that she was living all alone.

Mrs. Gunderson and Mrs. Bailey became close friends and many times, after the evening rush, Julie and the other waitresses would take a much needed break with the ladies. The two older women would talk about how life used to be and offer the kind of advice that only comes with age and experience to their young friends as they navigated life's problems and puzzles.

But today, Julie had off from work. It was December 20 and no mysterious parcel had shown up yet. As she had always received it by now, her heart sank a bit. It wasn't just because she wouldn't have that extra money for the wedding, but, perhaps even more so, because she realized that she might never find out the identity of her generous benefactor.

Ted and Jack had offered to watch Lucy and Ava so that Maggie could go with Julie to find a wedding gown. As Julie excitedly waited to be picked up, she looked around her tiny apartment in the Brownstone. The little tree stood merrily on the table by the window and lights twinkled from a wreath on the wall. She loved this place and it was rather bittersweet to think about leaving it. In just six short months she would be moving into Jack's condo. But life continually changes and even wonderful changes can bring hard moments.

Julie's phone dinged. A text from Maggie indicated she had arrived and so, grabbing her bright pink coat and her purse, she ran down the two flights of stairs. One thing I won't miss when I leave this place is the stairs, she thought smiling.

Julie and Maggie had a wonderful afternoon. Julie would try on a gown and Maggie, true friend that she was, would stand back carefully looking at every angle and then give her honest opinion. Maggie had become like a sister to Julie and this was of immeasurable value since she had no mom or sister to walk through this special time with her.

Julie had carefully tried on gowns that were in her $500 budget. And, while they were beautiful dresses, they just weren't quite right. They were too princessy or too garish. A few were just too plain and two or three were far too immodest.

At their last stop, a discount wedding shop, Julie's eyes rested on a simple, lace gown with a beaded overlay. It was perfect. She held her breath as she looked at the tag.

$1050.

She went through her wedding expenses in her mind to see if she could afford to spend that much on a gown. Where could I cut costs so that I can buy this gown? she mused.

As she was thinking about this, Maggie came up.

"Oh, Julie, that gown is gorgeous! It looks just like you."

"It does, doesn't it?" said Julie, longingly.

"Try it on!"

"But it's too expensive."

"Oh, just try it on. Here, give it to me," And she added it to the two or three she already held in her hand.

Julie saved the special dress for last when she went to the fitting room.

The first three were unimpressive. Finally, the satin and lace gown was pulled over head. Allowing the sales lady to button up the bodice in the back, Julie caught a glance of herself in the mirror. This was the dress. She just knew it.

As she stepped out of the fitting room, Maggie's eyes grew big.

"That's the dress." Her simple words confirmed what Julie herself was already thinking.

"That's how I feel, too. But I am just not sure I can afford it."

"You know, I want to check something. We were going to mark a few dresses on sale tomorrow and I think this may be one of them. I'll be right back," the kind sales lady went to the front of the store to check with her manager.

"Oh, wouldn't that be wonderful if it was?" breathed Maggie.

"It would indeed. But I don't want to get my hopes up," said Julie hesitantly, even though her hopes were already up.

Soon the lady returned with a big smile on her face. "This is one of the dresses! Tomorrow we are going to be running a special sale and this would take $100 off of the price. Would that help?"

Okay, so $100 was better than nothing. But that still made it close to $1000. Twice what her budget was.

"Would it be possible to hold this for me until tomorrow?" she asked. She just didn't want to spend that kind of money without talking to Jack first.

"Sure. I can hold it in the back for 48 hours according to our policy. After that, I will need to put it back out on the floor," she said kindly and then added, "I will just need some information from you."

They went up to the front to fill out a form and then Julie and Maggie were on their way home.

"I just wish I had the money to give to you, Jules, but with the kids in preschool and the furnace needing replaced, we just don't have it," said Maggie sadly.

"Oh, I would never expect that. I may be able to change my budget around a bit. Or maybe my anonymous Christmas gift will still show up this year," she said it jokingly.

"Well, you never know..." said Maggie hopefully.

"True. But it is always here by the beginning of December and here we are at December 20. It's okay. It was such a needed, life-changing blessing these past two years. God knew I needed that money at just that time. It helped me pay my living expenses when I had no idea where I would turn. And just think—I would never have met Ted on the street if I wouldn't have gone shopping that day which means I would never have met you. And even my nursing classes are because of my kind, anonymous friend. God has been so good to me and supplied my needs. And, let's face it, the wedding gown really isn't a need," Julie laughed.

Maggie smiled and then soon their conversation turned to the upcoming annual gingerbread house contest and other Christmas activities.

After grabbing a bite to eat, Maggie dropped Julie at her apartment.

She stopped in the brownstone's foyer to check her mail. In her box she found the familiar and welcome brown package. She blinked. Was she seeing things?

She held it tight in her hands as she ran delightedly up the two flights to her apartment. Her heart sang as she thought about the beautiful gown that she could now afford. Closing the door behind her, she breathlessly sat down to open it.

Tearing away the paper, she carefully opened the red and green plaid box that lay underneath the brown wrapping. There, in a bed of sparkly tissue paper, lay a small woodland couple holding an "engaged" sign. It was a special ornament to celebrate her recent engagement. Along with it came a cashier's check for $5000 dollars and a small typed note:

Dear Julie,

I hope this gift will help with wedding expenses. I will be praying for you and your fiancé as you plan your big day and will continue to pray for you both as you start your new life together. Best wishes!

Julie stood there absolutely stunned. She stared long and hard at the note, as if somehow this would reveal to her the answer she was looking for. But it was just a nondescript note. Black typed letters on plain white paper. There wouldn't be any answers there.

Five years had passed. Each December brought with it a special ornament. There was the small "First Christmas Together" ornament with the little bride and groom, and the little snow-covered cottage when Jack and Julie had moved from the condo to their craftsman-style home in the suburbs. And then there was a Baby's First Christmas ornament when Max had joined their family. Each year, the ornament was specially chosen to reflect some event or happening in her life. Other than that one exception the year before her wedding, the amount of money that came with the ornaments was always ten crisp $100 bills.

Julie reflected on this as she awkwardly moved to hang the ornaments on the tree. It was the day after Thanksgiving and she felt as big as a house. She lay her hand on her belly and felt a little kick. Max would soon be up from his nap and, at two years old, he was into everything. She sighed with exhaustion.

Over the past few years, life had brought much change. While she no longer worked at the restaurant, she was now holding a Bible Study there every Tuesday evening. It was so interesting how God had orchestrated its inception. She remembered it so clearly.

It was about three years ago now and Mrs. Bailey and Mrs. Gunderson were animatedly discussing what happens to a person after death, while Julie sat and listened. Mrs. Bailey was saying that Harold had believed the Bible and "all that jazz" about Jesus but she had never really thought there was anything to that.

Mrs. Gunderson laughed and said that Mr. Gunderson was sure nothing happened after you die and that that was the end. They went on for a while about how you just can't really know.

Julie, her heart beating fast, had finally spoken up. She told the women about the Bible and why she believed it to be true. She went on to explain how the only way to be reconciled to God was through Jesus Christ and she shyly offered to teach them more, if they were interested. She felt woefully inadequate to do this but she also realized that God had given her this special opportunity with these dear older friends. When they eagerly agreed, she asked Maggie to help her.

Thankfully, Maggie had been happy to join Julie in her new endeavor. Ted and Jack had offered to watch the kids, leaving the two young women free to meet with the ladies on Tuesday nights to explain to them the truths of scripture.

The small group had grown as Mrs. Bailey's friend from her book club, Lucinda, asked if she could join them. Soon after, Mrs. Gunderson's neighbor, Mrs. Littman, started coming. The group grew like this until there were about seven ladies who were committed to coming every week. Even Mrs. Zimmer, the little old Jewish lady who was a faithful customer at the restaurant, had expressed interest and had recently started to join them.

In a year or so, Mrs. Bailey placed her faith in Christ. Mrs. Gunderson still held off and Julie was getting a little discouraged. But she kept coming to the meetings so Julie and Maggie just kept praying for her.

Julie spotted her study Bible on the end table and the toys scattered on the floor. She smiled as she thought about how different her life was compared to seven years ago when she received that first mysterious package in the mail. A mommy and a Bible Study leader. Who would've guessed? And now twins. Twins! She wasn't sure if she could handle this but God was giving them to her, so she guessed He would give her the grace and strength to survive this.

She didn't know if they were boys or girls or one of each. Together, she and Jack, had decided to leave that as a surprise, just as they had done with Max.

She felt a sharp pain and sat down to rest. She wasn't due for another five weeks but now she wondered if these little ones would wait. The doctor had told her that twins often came early.

Julie grew increasingly uncomfortable until finally, a few days later, around midnight, they dropped a sleepy Max off at Ted and Maggie's and headed to the hospital.

Three weeks later found Julie and Jack back home with their arms full of babies. There had not been only two babies, but a third one hiding behind his sister. Two girls and a boy. Triplets! What a surprise! They had spent a few days in the NICU but they were all able to be home in time for Christmas.

They named the girls Kate and Kara. They named their new son Carson. Max was unsure what to think of all of these babies.

Life became a crazy carousel of feeding, changing, and rocking babies while still trying to make sure Max got the attention he needed. Thankfully, Jack's parents were a wonderful support and Martha McNally from the church had organized a schedule for church ladies to take shifts to help throughout most of the day and night.

December came and went in a blur. Somewhere in there, a new ornament arrived—a delicate porcelain ornament of three smiling babies wrapped up in mint green blankets, with the word "triplets" below it. The customary cash was with it. They could sure use those thousand dollars this year. Babies were expensive!

In a rare moment of silence with all the babies sleeping, Jack and Julie sat exhausted on the sofa by the twinkling tree. It was New Year's Eve and the new year promised to be an interesting one, to say the least.

Julie gazed at each ornament one by one that had come from what she was now calling her 'Christmas

Angel'. Her eyes landed on the latest one. The identity of the ornament-giver seemed almost irrelevant with all that was going on in her current life. Almost.

Somehow it was rather comforting to know that, out there somewhere, was someone who cared just a little bit about a grown woman who was, in all senses of the word, an orphan.

The kids were growing. Max was now a sturdy five-year-old and the triplets were three. Life had settled into a routine, albeit a very busy routine. Julie continued to receive the special ornaments along with the gift of a thousand dollars each December.

Each gift was welcome and needed, as money was always tight. Jack worked hard but with four kids to support, it was tough. There seemed to be an endless number of things needing fixed in their 1970s suburban home; their minivan, with over 180,000 miles on it, was constantly in need of repair; and the kids were always growing out of their clothing. Jack's paychecks were often spent before they had been received, despite their careful budgeting.

Although the Bible Study had ended upon the birth of the triplets, Julie had stayed in touch with Mrs. Bailey. She didn't go many places with the four kids because it was just so much work, but knowing that Mrs. Bailey didn't have any family to visit her, she'd take the kids over to visit the widow almost weekly to bring a little cheer into her life. The kids would create colored pictures to hang on her refrigerator and Julie would make homemade treats for her to munch on.

The family brought much comfort and joy to the childless lady who lived all alone in her small, lonesome apartment in the city.

One day, when Julie and the children stopped by to see her, a neighbor told her that Mrs. Bailey was gravely ill.

Julie dropped the kids off at Maggie's and then headed to the hospital. When she arrived, she found her sleeping peacefully.

She slid the room chair over by her bedside and sat down. Funny how God brought people into your life that you never expected. The Baileys had been a tremendous blessing in her life. Not only had they been so warm and friendly and opened up their small home to a lonely young girl, but since Mrs. Bailey became a believer, their relationship had grown deeper and more meaningful. The two women were true sisters now— sisters in Christ.

All of this came back to Julie, as she watched Mrs. Bailey's labored breathing. She thanked the Lord for her and reached out to hold her cold hand. She stirred and her eyes fluttered open.

"Julie? Is that you, dear?"

"It is, Mrs. Bailey."

"Thank you for coming to see me. It won't be long now until I see Harold."

"Oh, don't say that quite yet." Julie squeezed the old woman's hand.

"It's okay, my dear. I am ready to go, thanks to you. Harold knew the Lord and now we will be together in heaven because of Jesus. Only because of Him." She stopped to take a few labored breaths and then continued, "thank you, my dear Julie, for sharing the truth of God's Word with me. God was so good to bring you into my life. You are a dear girl."

Julie gave a wry smile at her use of the word "girl". She didn't feel much like a girl anymore but she supposed in Mrs. Bailey's eyes she would always be a girl.

Within a few minutes, Mrs. Bailey was sleeping peacefully again. A nurse told Julie that they didn't expect her to live much longer and so Julie called Jack to let him know that she'd be staying with Mrs. Bailey for a while.

She didn't want her to die without someone who loved her by her side. It just seemed important.

A few hours later, Mrs. Bailey had breathed her last and Julie had lovingly squeezed her hand one last time, as the tears freely flowed.

The weeks passed by and soon it was time to take down the Christmas tree. Jack was keeping the triplets busy with a craft and Max was playing with trucks by the fireplace, giving Julie some time to reflect as she lovingly held each mysterious ornament for a moment before carefully wrapping it for next year. There was the mini-globe, the wooden cross, and *Baby's First Christmas.* There was the miniature woodland couple, a tiny manger scene, the porcelain triplets, a glass cottage, and a beautifully crafted miniature bell that actually rang. Each one was special in its own way.

There had been no ornament this year and, to be honest, this had filled Julie with more sadness than even not getting the expected gift of money. The ornaments were so special and not getting one had made her Christmas feel incomplete.

She always hated taking down the tree. It seemed especially hard this year, with Mrs. Bailey's recent passing. Jack sensed her mood and brought her a cup of steaming coffee and told her to sit down for a few minutes. He rubbed her shoulders while she closed her eyes.

Suddenly, the doorbell rang. Max ran to the door and opened it to find the postman.

"I have a registered letter for your mama, young man. Is she here to sign it?"

Julie had soon signed for the letter and was sitting back on the sofa, looking at the mysterious letter.

Inside the envelope was a short note from a solicitor:

I have been instructed to send this letter to you upon the death of Mrs. Martha Bailey. I will be in touch with future instructions at a later date.

It was signed by a Mr. Brown, of Brown and Slade, a law firm from the city. She pulled out the short handwritten letter that accompanied the note.

Julie looked at the signature and saw that it was from Mrs. Bailey. She sat down on the nearby sofa to read it. Sensing that it was important, Jack took Max with him to check on the triplets so that she would have a few minutes alone to read it.

Julie unfolded the enclosed letter and read—

My dearest Julie,

For many years now, you will have been receiving an ornament each year, along with a gift of money. It has been my greatest pleasure to send these to you. I have so enjoyed watching you grow from a shy young girl into a capable young woman who loves the Lord and her family. You will never know how much you brightened these last few years of my life!

It is with this in mind that I bequeath all of my earthly belongings to you. While Harold and I settled down in a small apartment for our final years, you may not know that Harold was a very successful businessman. I have quite a tidy little sum that he saved up and I want you to have it. I ask that you give one third of it to worthy charitable causes that are Gospel-centered (I know, without a doubt, that you will do this with care). Please feel free to use the rest to care for your wonderful family.

I have watched you use the gifts I have sent you through the years in such a wise manner. I feel confident that you will do the same for this inheritance I am giving you. I know Harold would be pleased with my decision, as well. He loved you like he would have loved his own child.

And so have I. I couldn't have loved my own daughter more than I've loved you, should I have been blessed with one. Bless you, dear girl!

With much love,
Martha Bailey

Julie smiled as she thought of dear Mrs. Bailey. So she was her Christmas "angel" all of these years. She should have figured it out. But she was glad she hadn't. It had made it all the more special. So no more anonymous gifts or special ornaments. Her eyes brightened with unshed tears as she remembered how Mr. and Mrs. Bailey had blessed her so wonderfully through many years.

A few months later, the estate had been settled and Julie had given a third of it, about a million dollars, away to charities that she knew had the Gospel at the heart of their ministry. And then she put some of the money into savings for her children's college education and for whatever other needs came along. She and Jack loved their home and made the decision to stay there, despite having the means to move somewhere else. They did purchase a used SUV with less miles.

But Julie kept a good portion of it to start her own *Christmas Angel* fund. And each year she'd carefully pick a special Christmas ornament and send it on its way to someone in need, along with a gift of a thousand dollars.

It was in this way that Julie kept the spirit of Mrs. Bailey's generosity alive.

Christmas Comes
to Lupine Valley

It was getting dark and Henry still wasn't in from chores. Grace grabbed a wooden spoon and leaned over the big pot of stew that hung over the fire. A delicious fragrance wafted up from the pot as she stirred. Smiling, she reflected on the many meals she had made for her family at this hearth.

Henry and Grace had come to this valley thirty years ago now. She recalled that first view as they had come through the forest and looked down into this little valley. There, before them, was a meadow covered with shades of deep purple, lavender, and purply-pink. Wild lupines were blooming in all of their glory.

Henry had declared it the perfect place to build their new home, with the creek just a ways yonder and the large oak and maple trees that were scattered throughout the valley. Agreeing, Grace's eyes had sparkled as she told Henry that they would call their new home "Lupine Valley".

Lupine Valley had seen many changes over the years. Five children had been birthed there but only three lived to adulthood. Henry, jr. had been stillborn and her precious Sarah had died from Scarlet Fever when she was five years old. Even now, memories of this happy little girl brought tears to Grace's eyes. She brushed them away with her arm as she continued to stir.

The three remaining children were all grown now, living their own lives. Martha was married to the village's blacksmith and they were the parents to a large, lively brood. Jack had taken his young family and moved further west. They received only an occasional letter from him. Jane had gone east to live with her wealthy great aunt Ida for a time. They heard from her more often than they heard from Jack but it wasn't as often as Grace would have liked. Oh, how she missed her children and those busy days of motherhood. It was always worse around Christmastime.

"Enough of this!" she scolded herself and stood up and stretched. Reminding herself that Martha's family would be here for Christmas dinner, she smiled as she put her freshly made biscuits in a little basket on the table and then peered out into the darkness through the pane of glass at the front of the house. Henry's lantern swayed back and forth as he came in from the barn.

Suddenly, something else caught her eye way down towards the wood's edge. It looked to be beside the crick. It was a light of some sort. It disappeared. And then there it was again. What was that?

By this time, Henry had reached the small cabin and was stomping the dirt and debris from his boots. He opened the door and started talking about an infection on the leg of Star, their new mare.

"...should probably have Doc Hayfield take a look at it. Or do you know of some other remedy to try first? Not quite sure what to do."

Grace was still staring out the window and only heard the end of his sentence. With one final glance towards the woods, she sat down and put her mind to answering her husband's question about the horse and to serving him a well-deserved supper.

A half hour later, Henry leaned back and patted his stomach, "Oh, Grace, you sure do know how to cook. That was very, very good," he said the words heartily.

He pulled back from the table and went into the bedroom for his Bible so that they could have their evening read aloud of the scriptures together. Grace took this opportunity to look out the window and see if the light was still there. She stood there for a few moments, her eyes searching the darkness. Yes. There. There it was.

"Henry..."

By this time, he was seated with the open Bible, "What do you see so fascinating out that window, my dear?" he teased.

"Come look at this," she beckoned him to the window, "I see a light down by the crick. Am I imagining it?"

Henry pulled his spectacles off and put them on the table and then joined his wife at the window.

"There," she pointed towards the creek, "do you see it?"

"Hmmm, how strange," he said in his typical deliberate manner, "Maybe I'll go outside and see if I can figure out what it is," Henry was already pulling on his old brown coat. Soon he opened the door.

Grace hurried after him, wrapped in a thin shawl that wasn't very helpful in such cold weather. She stood there with her teeth chattering while Henry stared into the distance.

His face was sober as he said, "Go on inside, Grace. I am going to take a quick walk to the crick just to make sure all is well."

Grace looked at him. He looked worried and that made her worried. She had heard of bandits out this way but she never thought they'd come to Lupine Valley. They had always felt so safe and secure here.

They both went inside and Henry loaded his gun and then grabbed the lantern. He kissed Grace good-bye and gave her a squeeze, "Don't worry, sweetheart, I'll be okay," and, with that, he headed out the door.

Grace went to the window and watched him move quickly and stealthily towards the creek. When he was out of sight, she sat down in the rocking chair by the hearth and prayed.

Henry's heart pounded as he made his way down the path to the edge of the woods. The creek, splashing over and through the rocks, along with the wind swishing through the trees, helped to cover the sound of his footsteps. He followed the light which seemed to be on his side of the creek, up near the giant oak that spread its branches out over the water. The memory of the kids swinging off of that tree into the water many a hot summer day brought a quick, unbidden smile. In fact, it had come to be known as the "Swinging Tree".

As he crept closer he realized that the light was made by a fire. He carefully approached and stood behind the big oak. His eyes first spotted a small traveling bag and lantern on the ground nearby. The lantern would explain the moving light. Its owner probably had been using it earlier when Grace looked out the window. As his eyes lifted and focused in on the fire and the lone person who sat beside it, they grew wide with surprise.

A young woman—why she looked younger than his own Jane—sat on a log with her hands and feet towards the fire, looking both hopeless and exhausted. As he was deciding how to handle this odd situation, he saw her shift her weight in an ungainly manner and suddenly realized that she was very pregnant. He stood there helplessly for a moment and then realized: His wife would know what to do. He'd see if he could convince the girl to go up to the house to see Grace.

He didn't want to scare her, so he moved a bit closer and then cleared his throat. She startled and fear leaped into her eyes. He stepped out of the shadows.

"Ummm, ma'am, hello there. My name is Henry and me and my wife, well, uhhh, we live in the cabin up the hill over that way," he pointed towards the speck of friendly light that could just barely be made out through the woods, "Are you okay, ma'am?"

His words, spoken humbly and so kindly, made the girl feel safe. And then the tears started to flow. She seemed unable to stop them. Henry stood awkwardly by, unsure of what to do. He wished now that he would have brought Grace along. But, of course, he never expected to find a pregnant girl by herself when he had set out a few minutes ago.

"Are you alone?" He asked gently.

She nodded her head, as a new wave of tears took over. He sat down on a nearby tree trunk and waited patiently. Being married for over thirty years and having daughters to boot, he knew womenfolk sometimes just had to have a good cry.

When she started to settle down he asked her if she would like to come up to the cabin to get warm. His wife always had a ready pot of tea in the evening and she looked like she could use a cup.

She hesitated for just a moment before nodding her head ever so slightly. Pulling her woolen shawl on more tightly, she picked up the small bag and lantern that Henry had spotted earlier. By the looks of things, that baby could come any day. Henry couldn't help but wonder what she was doing out here all alone by his creek.

He offered to take her bag, which she willingly handed to him, and then held his lamp up nice and high to give plenty of light as they walked up the dark path through the woods and out into the meadow. There the moon shone brightly and it was easier to see. Soon they were at the little cabin and opened the door.

Grace's heavy heart lifted as she saw her husband come through the door. But what a surprise to see a very pregnant girl follow him in. Why, she looked to be no more than sixteen!

"Well, my dear Grace, you weren't seeing things. I found this young woman down at the Swinging Tree, warming herself by a fire."

"Oh, my goodness! Oh, dear girl, come and sit by the fire," Grace drew her towards the rocking chair by the cozy fire.

The girl lowered herself carefully onto the plump cushion that Grace had handmade for the hard wooden seat. It felt heavenly after what she had been through for the past couple of days.

Grace busied herself in getting the girl a cup of hot tea. She swirled a bit of honey in it before handing it to her.

The girl put her hands around it and sighed deeply. "Thank you," she said, her eyes shining with unshed tears, as she took a sip of the hot liquid. She didn't say any more and, after just a few moments, set the tea down on the hearth, leaned back in the chair, and closed her eyes.

Grace pulled back and whispered to Henry, "The poor thing is exhausted. Let's just make a bed up for her and let her sleep. We can find out more tomorrow."

Henry agreed and so Grace went into the girls' bedroom to prepare it for their guest.

Soon the girl was sleeping peacefully in the comfortable bed in the cozy cabin.

As Grace peeped in on her for the umpteenth time, Henry laughed, "she's not going to disappear."

Grace gave a wry smile, "She's just so young. I wonder what her story is."

"I am sure we will find out in the morning."

And with that they blew out the candle on the table and went to bed, too.

The following morning, Henry and Grace quietly ate breakfast while the girl slept. Oh, how exhausted she must have been.

When Grace peeked in on her after breakfast, she was just waking up.

"Good morning!" Grace said cheerfully, "I hope you slept well. I took the liberty to wash a few things in your bag so you'd have something clean and fresh to wear today. It dried so nicely by the fire overnight. We can wash the rest of your clothing today in some nice, hot water," and with those words, she laid a dress, along with some fresh underclothing, on the chair in the corner of the room and then quietly left, closing the door behind her.

Soon the girl came out of the bedroom wearing the clean dress and a shy smile.

"Are you hungry?"

She nodded her head and sat down at the table, where hot coffee and delicious-looking flapjacks sat waiting.

Grace sat quietly by the hearth as she waited for the girl to finish eating. She tried not to look impatient but inside she was chomping at the bit to hear the girl's story.

Finally, the girl turned to her, "Thank you so much, ma'am. That was delicious."

"You are quite welcome. Do you feel up to talking this morning?"

The girl sighed, "Yes. I guess I do owe you my story after all you've done for me."

Grace gave her the comfortable rocker and then pulled a chair close by. She asked her a question to get her started, "Let's start at the beginning, shall we? What is your name?"

"Clara. Clara Hill."

"And how old are you? Do your parents know where you are?" Grace asked gently.

"I am twenty. And I am actually on the way to my parents. Maybe I should start at the beginning," she said and then continued, "A couple of years ago, I got married to Edward Hill. We grew up together. He wanted adventure—Eddy always wanted adventure for his whole life—and so we got on a train and headed west. We didn't get that far before we ran into some troubles we didn't see comin'. We were soon out of the little bit of money we had saved and so Eddy found a job in Slate Valley and that's where we stayed put."

Grace recognized the name of the town that was about 20 miles northwest of them.

"Mama and Papa weren't very happy that I was moving so far away, but I was full of adventure myself and excited to go," Clara sighed and then continued, "Everything went okay for a while. Until earlier this year when Eddy was drafted."

Grace remembered that there had been a draft for World War I last May for the young men in the country. It hadn't affected her or her family but Clara's predicament reminded her of how many must have been affected.

Clara went on to explain that a few months after she realized she was pregnant, Eddy had left for the War. She had lived a lonely, friendless life in a few rooms above the general store. When she had gotten behind on her rent by a month and couldn't pay yet again last week, the landlord told her she had to be out by the following day. He didn't seem to care that her husband was fighting for the country nor consider her physical condition.

Grace's mouth fell open. How could anyone be so cruel?

Clara continued matter-of-factly, "The day after that happened, I received word that my husband was missing in action," she tried to say it without emotion but gave a little pause to catch the sob in her throat and wipe her eyes with the back of her hand, "At that point, I just didn't know what to do. I didn't mind living there when it was Eddy and me. But being there without Eddy and knowing he was probably never coming back and, with no money and even no place to live, well, it just seemed time to go home.

So I packed a bag along with a bit of food and decided to try to get to Mama and Papa before this little one makes its appearing. It's only a few hundred miles and I figured I might find a little help along the way. But it may not have been so smart to do that with the baby coming and all." She finished with a big, hopeless sigh.

"When do you expect your little one?"

"I really don't know," she shrugged her shoulders. With some tactful questioning, Grace realized that she hadn't had seen a doctor or midwife up to this point.

But, in a quick evaluation of her condition with her limited experience, Grace wondered how wise it was for Clara to be traveling anywhere right now.

"Surely there is a church in your town? Did you ever reach out to the pastor? Or some of the church ladies? Surely, they would have helped you."

Clara grew a bit uncomfortable at this point and Grace was sorry she had mentioned it. Finally, she said, "I'm not really a church kind of girl and those church ladies always seemed like real snobs when I saw them in town."

Grace tucked that knowledge away for later and then asked, "So how did you end up here in our woods?"

"Well, I was traveling on the road from Oak Ridge when it started to grow dark. I saw your lane and it looked so friendly-like, that I thought maybe I could find a cozy place to rest for the night. I saw that little path and then found that old tree by the crick and, well, it looked pretty safe there. I am so sorry if I am causing you any trouble," she looked genuinely worried about this.

"Oh, my dear, we are so glad you are here and want to help you. It seems like you've had a very rough few months," Grace's comforting words fell over Clara like a soothing balm.

"You know, God is in the business of meeting needs. Just look at how He brought you right to us in Lupine Valley!"

Clara wasn't sure she agreed with Grace, but she smiled politely.

Grace continued, "The first thing we need to do is write a letter to your parents, letting them know you are coming home and to expect you. I don't know exactly how yet, but we are going to get you home."

Grace pulled out a piece of paper and a fountain pen from a shelf above the little desk they kept in the corner. She invited Clara to come and sit down to write.

"In the meantime, we are going to have Henry send them a telegram so they know you are safe."

Clara looked down at the ground and seemed embarrassed, until finally Grace realized she probably couldn't write. Scolding herself, she kindly said to her, "Why don't you tell me what you want to write?"

The next few moments were spent with Clara dictating a short but meaningful letter to her parents telling them she was coming home. Grace folded it, put it in an envelope, and then addressed it with the information Clara gave her.

Leaving the young woman sitting by the hearth, she pulled on her shawl and took the letter out to Henry, where he was chopping wood.

"Could you take this to the post office and then send off a telegram to them, as well? If it was Martha or Jane, I'd want to know they were okay," as a mother herself, she wanted Clara's parents to know as soon as possible that their daughter was in safe hands and that they would figure out a way to get her home.

Henry said he would finish cutting the wood and then head out. And, true to his word, he was headed to town in the horse and wagon within the hour.

The next few weeks flew by as Christmas Day rapidly approached. Henry and Grace invited Clara to stay with them until the baby was born and she agreed that would be best. She had received a telegram from her parents, stating they would pay for her fare home when the baby was old enough to travel. With this settled, Clara was able to enjoy the holiday season as she settled comfortably into the little, pleasant cottage in Lupine Valley.

Grace had many opportunities to share with Clara about the baby that came that first Christmas night. She explained how baby Jesus would grow up to die for the sins of man and that, through Jesus, anyone could be forgiven of their sins and be reconciled to God. Clara didn't say much, but she did listen. She hadn't ever heard the story of Christmas put quite like that before and it gave her much pause for thought. Meanwhile, Henry and Grace prayed that she would come to know the Lord Jesus personally, contemplating that perhaps this was the reason for their special Christmas guest.

Clara joined Grace in all of her many holiday activities, although she grew noticeably more tired as Christmas Day approached.

On the day before Christmas Eve, Henry drove the two women into town to make some cookie deliveries. They had made dozens and dozens of cookies the day before and now it was time to deliver them. The festive plates of cookies, wrapped with red bows, bounced up and down as Henry carefully guided the wagon to town.

They first stopped at the church parsonage, where Pastor Marten was studying for his Christmas sermon.

"Oh, Grace, what a lovely gift! Mabel's rheumatism has been acting up and she wasn't up to making cookies this year, so your gift is appreciated even more than usual!" He said with a twinkle in his eye as he rubbed his ample belly.

Grace asked after his family and they spoke a few more pleasantries before she joined Henry and Clara back at the wagon. The doctor's office was next on their list.

Henry carefully helped Clara off the wagon here so that the Doctor could give her a quick check-up. Thankfully, he was there when they knocked on the door.

"Well, what have we here? No baby, yet, Clara?" He laughed.

"Not yet, Doctor Miller," Clara's voice reflected the fatigue she felt in every bone of her body.

"Well, by the looks of it, I'd expect that young'un any day now!" The friendly doctor gratefully took the large plate of cookies from Grace and then gave Clara a quick examination. Announcing that all looked well, he sent them on their way, assuring them that he'd be seeing them again soon.

After stops to deliver cookies to the Widow Burgess, elderly Mr. and Mrs. Whitley, and several other townspeople, they finally drove the wagon to Martha's house with the last two plates of their cookies.

"Oh, Mom, thank you for these! I just wish I could have helped you make them this year! I didn't even have time to make any for my own family," Her broad smile showed that she didn't mind too terribly much.

Motherhood suited her. Martha loved to bake cookies but she loved being a mama even more. With two-month-old twins added to her other four, all who were under the age of eight, it was just a little too much to help this year.

During their visit, Grace happened to look up and see Clara looking a bit pale as she held tightly on to her belly with her eyes closed. She made her way over to Henry and whispered in his ear. He nodded and announced that it was time to go.

James and John, Martha's two oldest boys, protested loudly, "Awwww, but you just got here, Grandpa!"

Henry quietly leaned down and said something. The boys looked over at Clara and nodded their heads quite seriously. They understood.

Martha told Grace that if they needed her, she could come. Harvey would gladly stay with the kids in an emergency. Grace smiled gratefully and, in a flurry of good-bye hugs and kisses, they climbed in their wagon.

Clara grew more and more uncomfortable with each bump and shake of the wagon as it made its way back to Lupine Valley. Grace tried to make her as comfortable as possible but there was little she could do.

When they arrived home, Clara announced that she was going to go lay down.

Grace was uncertain. Had Clara's labor officially begun? Or was she coming down with that flu bug that was going around? Finally, she went into the room with a cup of hot tea to see if she could find out.

"How are you feeling, dear?"

"Awful. Just awful. I have such a back ache," she rubbed her lower back as she spoke.

"Are the pains coming with any regularity?"

"No, not really."

"Okay. Here is some hot tea. Please call for me if you need anything," she gave Clara's hand a gentle squeeze.

"Okay," she said feebly.

The day passed by quietly, with Grace checking on her every hour or so. The pains did start becoming more regular as the evening wore on, indicating that she was indeed in labor, so Grace shooed Henry off to bed and decided to sleep in the rocking chair. She had just dozed off when she heard a loud cry. She jumped up, trying to figure out where she was, when she suddenly remembered. Clara!

She ran into her room to see her thrashing about on the bed in pain.

"I think it's soon time," she said, gasping for breath.

Grace ran out of the room to tell Henry to fetch the doctor. He was soon saddled up and riding towards town.

Meanwhile, she tried to remember everything she could about a baby's birthing. After setting a pot of water on the fire to boil and finding some clean cloths, she went and sat by Clara's bedside to wait for the doctor.

Thankfully, Henry was soon at the door with Doctor Miller.

"Well, Miss Clara, are you ready to be a mama?"

Clara smiled wanly.

Henry waited impatiently in the main room, while Grace and the doctor aided Clara in the bedroom.

An hour later, he heard a loud cry. Grace soon peeked her head out the door.

"Is all well?" he asked anxiously. The girl had become like another daughter to him in just the few weeks she had been staying with them.

Grace gave a huge smile as she affirmed that it was. "It's a healthy baby boy. She is naming him Edward Henry, after his missing father and after you, my dear," Grace said with delight.

Henry was shocked and delighted to hear this. What a wonderful Christmas surprise.

As Christmas Eve dawned, the people in the cottage in Lupine Valley were a happy, exhausted bunch. There is nothing quite like a new baby at Christmastime.

Christmas Day dawned bright and clear. Grace was fixing breakfast while Clara sat on the rocking chair, watching the fire. Baby Edward lay sleeping in the old cradle that Henry had retrieved from the barn loft and then tenderly cleaned and polished.

Conversation flowed freely between the two women as Grace set the table. In the center she placed a small and treasured Christmas figurine of Joseph, Mary, and baby Jesus.

"How nice to have our own Christmas baby this year," she said happily.

Clara looked over at the cradle where her baby lay and smiled. She already loved him more than life itself. Her smile dimmed as she remembered that he would grow up without his father. The thought of this made her heart so heavy. Imperceptibly, she gave her head a little shake. She wouldn't think about that today. After all, it was Christmas Day and she would soon be leaving these new and dear friends who had been so kind to her. She wanted to enjoy this day. There would be plenty of time to think about the future tomorrow.

"I wonder why Henry isn't in from the barn yet," Grace went to the window to look out, "Well, I'll be..."

"What is it?"

"Someone is outside with Henry. Who in the world would come visiting on Christmas? I hope nothing happened at the McCullough farm," Grace worried as she thought of the large, needy family that lived about a mile from them.

Henry hurried towards the house. A stranger, left arm hanging useless and awkwardly at his side, walked beside him. It definitely wasn't Mr. McCullough.

Grace went to the door and opened it for the two men. As they walked through the door, a loud and joyful cry was heard.

"Eddy?! Eddy!" Clara leaped off the chair, despite the fact that she had just had a baby.

Eddy and Clara were in each other's arms in seconds. Henry and Grace looked on wonderingly. Why, it was their own Christmas miracle.

Clara, with tears streaming down her face, finally spoke. "I thought you were dead, Oh, Eddy, I thought I'd never see you again. How did you find me?"

Eddy held on to his wife tightly until he spotted the cradle.

"Is this our baby?" He said with awe. He moved to the cradle and gently bent down to touch the little hand that had flung itself out of the blanket.

"Meet Edward Henry," Clara said proudly and then she added, "We may want to call him Henry now that his daddy is around."

"Henry is a right fine name," He looked at Henry appreciatively as he said these words.

"Come, come, let's eat breakfast. There is plenty," Grace's words encouraged them to the table where a veritable Christmas feast was laid out before them. Bacon, sausage, eggs, flapjacks, and sweet rolls all gave off a wonderful fragrance, while a basket that held a few big oranges sat nearby. This treat had become a Christmas tradition and Grace always looked forward to her first bite into the luscious, round fruit.

Henry thanked the Lord for the food and then, as Grace poured cups of strong coffee, Eddy started to fill them in on how he came to be with them on Christmas Day.

His division had been fighting the enemy on French soil when he had become injured. He had been knocked out cold and, in the fray of the chaotic retreat from the battle, he had been left for dead. When he awoke he found himself in the home of a family who lived high in the mountains. Though they couldn't speak a word of English, the family both protected and nursed him. He spoke of them fondly as he explained that it took several months to recover from his injuries.

"Unfortunately, my arm will never be the same," he said this soberly as he looked at the helpless limb hanging by his side.

"I don't care. I am just glad you are here. That's all that matters," Clara stated this with fervor.

Eddy smiled tenderly at her and then continued. He had stayed with the family until just a month ago, when he was finally able to communicate with the war office that he was alive and needed to get home.

When he arrived home, it was to find out that Clara was no longer there and had not even received the information that he was still alive. Not knowing what to do, he had traveled to her parents, hoping to find her there. Thankfully, they had heard from her just a few weeks earlier and could tell him exactly where she was. When Eddy had arrived at Oak Ridge that Christmas morning, he had knocked on the door of the church parsonage where Pastor Marten knew immediately who he was talking about and had kindly directed him to his little family staying in Lupine Valley.

Clara sighed with contentment, "I still can't believe you are here."

The rest of Christmas Day was spent in joyous celebration. It was a special day to be remembered by all.

Late in the afternoon, Henry brought the wagon around, so that he and Grace could head into town to have dinner with Harvey and Martha. Eddy and Clara decided to stay home with baby Henry and enjoy some time together as a family.

As Henry and Grace made their way to town, they went over their exciting day. To think that Eddy was still alive and reunited with his little family! How amazing!

Little did they know that they had their own surprise in store.

They were soon in front of Harvey and Martha's house. James and John, with little Millie not far behind them, came out shouting "Grandpa! Grandma!"

But who was this? Another child stood shyly in the doorway. Why, was that their granddaughter, Caroline, all grown-up? But no. It couldn't be!

"Mom! Dad! Surprise!" And out rushed their son, their daughter-in-law, along with their three children. And, there, behind them, stood Jane!

Grace's eyes welled up with joyful tears as she surveyed the happy group before her.

With smiles and laughter, they told Henry and Grace how they had been planning this special reunion all year.

Christmas dinner was crowded and oh, so noisy and Henry and Grace loved every second of it.

Soon, it was time to go home. Many happy plans were made for the coming days and, with assurances of seeing one another again soon, they took their leave.

As they drove home under a clear sky full of stars, Grace sighed contentedly, "I believe this is the happiest Christmas I have ever had."

"I sure do agree with you, my dear! God is so good."

And with those words, Henry reached his strong arm around Grace and hugged her as the horses led the wagon back to the little cottage in Lupine Valley.

Epilogue—

Eddy, Clara, and little Henry left a few weeks later. They had become like part of the family during those weeks and Henry and Grace watched them go with sad hearts. Letters and visits were promised as they gave each other parting hugs.

Henry had placed a well-worn Bible in Eddy's hands before they left.

"Young man, this has been an invaluable and irreplaceable source of guidance to me here on earth, as well as showing me how I can be saved for all eternity. I hope that you will read it and take it seriously."

Eddy took it soberly and promised he would.

As Henry and Grace watched them climb into the train, it was with hope in their hearts that they would soon be part of the family of God.

"We'll just have to keep praying for them. God is so faithful," said Grace.

Henry squeezed Grace's hand as they started off for home. It had been a Christmas never to be forgotten in Lupine Valley.

An Extraordinary Christmas: Christmas Comes to Lupine Valley

The Lost Son

Dear Belinda—

I hope this finds you well. We are settling into our new normal with baby Charlie. He loves Ned and just lights up when he comes in the room. I want you to know that we are happy to keep him for as long as you need us to. Please be in touch when things settle down and we will figure out how to get him across the country. Perhaps Ned and I could take a road trip. We have always wanted to do that. Take care.

Love Always,
Harriet

Abby stared at the letter in her hand. The box of letters from Grandma's attic had so far been boring accounts of daily life with an occasional memorable happening thrown in. They were filled with lists of canned fruits and vegetables, illnesses of farm animals, and neighborhood events. Most were from Grandma's sister, Edna, in Omaha; a few were from her sister-in-law, Martha, in Canada; and then there were just a handful that were from her grandma's best friend from childhood, Harriet, who lived in Oregon. The biggest surprise up to this point had been a beautiful love letter penned by her grandfather, a staid and quiet man who

112

rarely shared his feelings. At least that had been the biggest surprise until right now.

Abby looked again at the shocking letter in her hand. Her eye caught another letter tucked into the large brown envelope from which she had drawn this first one. She carefully pulled it out and unfolded it. The date was five years after the first one had been written.

Dear Belinda,

I hope this finds you well. We haven't heard from you for a while and I am a bit worried about you. It is hard to believe Charlie is going to be six years old next spring. He has become part of our family and the girls just dote on him. It's been fun having a boy in the family and we thank you for sharing him with us.

I do think it may be good to settle in on a plan for Charlie as we move into the future. It's been five years and we all feel rather in limbo. Do you still plan to raise him now that things have simmered down and Felix is no longer in the picture? Each year we wait will make it harder on us and on Charlie. I guess I am just a bit confused but will wait to hear from you.

Love,
Harriet

Abby peered into the brown envelope, hoping for more letters to explain. But there were none. She then shuffled through the rest of the unread letters still in the old wooden box. She desperately wanted to solve the mystery she had just stumbled upon. But the only other letters to be found from Harriet were when she had gone away to camp one summer as a teenager.

Abby thought of her kind and cheerful grandmother who had just recently moved in with her mom due to some health issues. Did Grandma have a son out west somewhere? Or was there some other explanation? Who was Charlie?

"Mom! Preston took my doll!" a voice called Abby from the past and back to her little cottage on Willow Lane.

"Preston...!" Abby called as she pushed her chair back from the small vintage desk in front of her and went to tend to her children.

A few minutes later, with Preston, Kyle, and Maddy in front of a familiar movie and munching on goldfish crackers, Abby headed back to her desk to see if she could find out more about the mysterious Charlie. She felt a little guilty leaving the kids in front of the TV but she figured for this once it wouldn't hurt. She didn't do it often.

Sitting back down at her desk, she stared out the window and thought of what had just come to light. What other conclusion could be drawn but that her grandmother had had a son named Charlie? It appeared that, instead of bringing him with her when she moved east to marry Grandpa, she had left him in Oregon with her best friend, Harriet.

Had Grandma Belinda kept Charlie a secret from everyone? Or did Grandpa know about Charlie? Was Charlie still alive? If so, where was he? Did he know he had family here in Ohio?

The many questions came like a flood, begging to be answered. Abby looked at her watch. It was time to start dinner. The questions would have to wait.

After dinner, and with the kids playing a game with John at the kitchen table, Abby went back to her desk and picked up the first letter and stared at it for a few moments. Picking up the cell phone that lay on her desk, she clicked on her mom's number.

"Hello?"

"Hey, Mom. How are you this evening?"

"Just fine, dear. Grandma and I were just sitting here talking. Dad is out doing something in the garage. Hanging some new rack or other. You know how important it is that he stay organized," she laughed.

Abby looked at her watch. It was only 7pm. Should she or shouldn't she?

She took a deep breath and dove right in, "Mom, can I come by to talk to you and Grandma for a few moments? Won't take long."

Her parents lived a short ten minutes away. She could easily be home before the kids' bedtime routine.

"Sure, honey. Should I be worried?" Her mom sounded a bit unnerved by the solemnity in Abby's voice, which she tried, in vain, to hide.

"Oh, no," Abby nervously laughed, "I'll be there shortly."

She clicked to end the conversation and sat there for a brief moment, praying that the Lord would give her wisdom. She then went to John and asked to talk to him. They left the kids playing the game without him for just a moment while she explained what she had found earlier that day.

He whistled through his lips and then exclaimed, "Whoah!"

"I know, right?"

"I can understand that you want to know what's going on, but do you really want to bring this up as we head into the holiday season? Maybe we should wait until the new year?" John rubbed his left ear, as he had a habit of doing in uncertain situations.

"You are rubbing your ear," Abby smiled at him, breaking the tension of the moment. He grinned as she continued on in a more serious tone, "you might be right. But it's too late now. I know about Charlie and the new year feels like an eternity away at this moment," she paused briefly and then said, "Why don't I go over and just see how it goes? Ask a couple of questions and see where they lead? I won't bring it up if it just doesn't seem like the right time. I promise."

John agreed and soon Abby was on her way.

As she pulled into the driveway, she saw both her mom and grandma waving cheerily from the living room window, heads together and smiling broadly. She hoped they would still be smiling when she left.

Pulling her coat tightly around her, she walked briskly to the door in the nippy night air which was reminding her that winter was right around the corner.

Gathering around Abby with warm hugs and peppering her with questions about her week and John and the kids consumed the first fifteen or twenty minutes. Both her mom and her grandma loved exuberantly and without condition.

Abby wasn't necessarily scared to have the upcoming conversation with them but she was reluctant.

As the conversation about current happenings wound down, the room grew awkwardly quiet.

"Are you okay, dear?" It was Grandma who finally broke the silence, "you don't seem quite yourself."

"I was just thinking that, as well." Both sets of inquiring and concerned eyes fixed themselves on her.

Squirming a bit, Abby tried to decide how to handle this. It wasn't going anything like she had hoped. Oh, why couldn't she hide her feelings better? Frustrated and never being one to "beat about the bush", she made the impromptu decision to just say what was on her mind.

"Grandma, do you remember when we had that conversation about me helping to sort through all of the stuff left in your house?"

"I sure do. And I am so blessed that you would help me with that. It is such a huge and overwhelming task. I could never do it all by myself," Grandma Belinda smiled with gratitude.

"Well, there was a wooden box of letters in the attic that I brought home to read through..."

When Abby mentioned the wooden box, Grandma's face grew white as a sheet.

"Mom! Are you okay?" cried Janet, running to her mother's side.

"I am fine, dear. Please sit back in your chair," the pallor of her face belied her faint words.

Janet walked back to her chair, her mind in a whirl.

"I cannot believe that I forgot about that box," Grandma Belinda said the words casually but her breath was raspy, revealing the magnitude of this moment.

"So you know what I found then," Abby said this in a low, gentle voice.

Tears started to form in her grandmother's eyes as the secret that had been hidden in her heart for over fifty years came to light.

"You learned about Charlie, then?" She said softly.

"Charlie? Who is Charlie?" Janet was beside herself with concern and curiosity by now and wanted to understand what was happening between her daughter and her mother.

"I guess that is what I am here to find out," said Abby.

Grandma Belinda put her face in her hands as she started quietly weeping, her shoulders shaking.

Janet handed her mother a box of tissues as she asked, "Abby, what is going on?"

Abby pulled the two letters out of her purse and handed them to her mom. Janet took them, her eyes growing wide in disbelief as she read them.

"I have a brother? Is that what this means?"

Grandma Belinda sighed, "a half-brother, yes," she said the words with defeat and perhaps just a touch of relief. The secret was finally out.

Abby and Janet quietly waited for her to continue.

"I will tell you the story. I should have told you a long time ago," said Grandma, as she started to reveal the decades-old secret that had haunted her for most of her life.

Abby could feel the tension in the room. She glanced at her mom, who was sitting stiffly on the striped blue chair. Her back was straight and her mouth was tight as she waited for her mother to reveal the details surrounding the brother she never knew she had.

Grandma gave a shaky sigh and then continued, "I am not proud of this part of my life. The first twenty-five years of my life were...well, let me just start at the beginning."

Janet tried to think of what she knew about her mother's life prior to her birth. Come to think of it, she didn't know very much.

"I had a wonderful childhood with parents who loved me. And my neighbor, Harriet, was always my best friend. But when I was around fifteen, I started hanging around with a new friend. Patty was not the kind of girl any parent would want their daughter to hang out with and my parents were not very happy. I am not really sure what drew me to Patty. I guess it was because she was popular and fun and, at that point in my life, that was all that really mattered to me. Anyway, Patty and I struck up a friendship and she was the one who introduced me to her cousin, Felix."

Ahhh, the mysterious Felix mentioned in the letter. What did that letter say? That he was "out of the picture"... Abby remembered.

Grandma Belinda continued while the other women sat quietly listening, "Felix was bad news from the beginning. But I was young and dumb and he was so handsome and charming," she smiled wryly, remembering the young man.

"Felix was one of those guys that could charm the mittens off of someone freezing in the wintertime. He could talk anyone into anything. But, underneath all of that charm and charisma, unbeknownst to me was a darker, uglier Felix. But I am getting ahead of myself."

"At any rate, Felix was an older boy. He worked at the local garage, pumping gas, and he took a liking to me. I was so enamored. I couldn't believe this older, handsome boy would ever choose me. I was a plain and rather boring sort of girl. I had wondered who would ever choose one such as I and, lo and behold, this boy did! You can see how I was so easily infatuated and then deceived..." her voice faded, remembering.

Abby, considering her grandmother's large brown eyes and curly chestnut hair, now graying with age, couldn't imagine anyone thinking her plain. She tried to picture her grandmother as a young woman but she hadn't opened Grandma's photo box from the attic yet and she couldn't recall ever seeing any photos on display.

"Soon Felix and I became an 'item', as they used to say in those days and much to my parents' dismay. I know they didn't know what to do. A few months after we started dating, tragedy struck."

Janet dug back into her memory, vaguely remembering that she had never met her maternal grandparents because of an accident.

"My parents were walking to church on a beautiful Sunday morning when a drunk driver swerved on to the sidewalk, instantly killing them both. He had been out at the local bar all night and was on his way home," her eyes brightened with unshed tears as she shared this.

"I will always regret that I was not right with them when they were taken home to be with the Lord. They were so disappointed in me and that's how they left this earth—filled with disappointment at their youngest child's foolish escapades," she sighed deeply.

"You would think that this event would have put me back on the right path, but it didn't. Instead, in my desperation and hopelessness, I made some really bad choices. Finding myself without a place to live and ignoring my sister's plea to come live with her, as well as the kind invitation of my Aunt Betty, I moved into an apartment with Patty. I guess I was rather excited to be free to do what I wanted. But, there, without the watchful eye of my parents or any other wiser and older adults, I found solace and comfort in Felix's arms and finally gave in to his pressure to...well, you know," her face grew a bit red at this vague confession.

Abby and Janet exchanged glances as she continued, "Soon I found out I was pregnant. This was when the real trouble began. Felix was always selfish but, after this, he grew mean. He wanted me to get rid of the child but I refused. His abuse soon moved from verbal to physical and I was beat up pretty badly more times than I can count."

Janet's caught her breath. All this had happened to her sweet and kind mother. How could she not have known?

Grandma Belinda looked at Janet with clear eyes, as if knowing what she was thinking and said quietly, "it's okay. You couldn't have known. I didn't want you to know."

Janet asked the question that had been gnawing at her since this had first come to light, "Did Dad know?"

Grandma Belinda sighed, "well, not at first. But I did tell him eventually. But I'll get to that," she continued her story, "the uglier Felix became, the more sure I became that I needed to get away from him. But he didn't want to let me go. So you can see how this went. I had no home, no support. He wanted me but only under two conditions: No marriage and no children.

I actually moved in with Felix, believing he would change and eventually want to marry me. Back in those days, this branded me as a very loose woman. I still can't believe I actually did such a thing but I felt so lost and alone," she hung her head.

120

She wiped her eyes and blew her nose on the crumpled tissue she was holding tightly in her hand and then continued, "I hung around for a while, thinking that the baby would soften Felix's heart, but it actually got worse when Charlie arrived. It was one thing for me to be the recipient of Felix's abuse but when baby Charlie became a target, I knew it was time to leave."

Abby's heart ached, thinking of this young, forlorn woman making a choice to escape a man who was set on hurting her and her child.

"I guess I should mention here that Felix did have good days. The abuse wasn't constant. And he'd always promise to change. I guess that's what kept me there for so long."

She continued on, "by this time my sister, Edna, had moved to Omaha and my brother, Carl, had moved to Canada. The only safe person I could think of nearby was my Aunt Betty. And she is who I finally turned to for help."

Janet remembered Aunt Betty. She knew that her mom had had a very special relationship with her while she was alive but she had never understood why.

"Aunt Betty took me in and was like a lioness in protecting me. She had been so worried about me and gladly supported me in my desire to change my life. I will forever be in her debt. It was Aunt Betty who suggested I give Charlie up for adoption but I just couldn't do it. However, somewhere inside of me, I knew that Charlie needed some stability in his life and I needed to get a job. Aunt Betty was unable to watch him while I worked due to a chronic illness so, finally, in desperation, I asked Harriet and her husband, Ned, to consider taking him in. I knew this was a lot to ask, but they gladly welcomed my sweet boy into their little family. This seemed like the best option— not final, like an adoption, and yet getting him into a stable home while I tried to put the pieces of my life back together."

"I found a job at the local shoe factory and that is where I met your father, Janet," she looked at her beloved daughter, "He was everything Felix was not. He wasn't dashing or charismatic but, instead, very staid and stable. He was handsome enough but in a rugged way, rather than the dark, brooding way Felix had been. These things drew me to him. He was also a godly man. He insisted on me attending church with him and, soon, I was back in fellowship with the Lord, after all those long years. Honestly, I believe this is when I was actually saved. It really wasn't until that time that I understand that I was a sinner without hope and understood my need for Christ to save me."

She stopped for a moment in deep reflection.

"I did not tell Marvin about my past. I was so ashamed. All he knew was that my parents had died and that I had been in an abusive relationship in my past and that I still feared this man. I didn't offer much more than that. When I introduced him to Harriet and Ned, I introduced Charlie as their son," she smiled wryly, "I am actually surprised he never said anything because Charlie was the spitting image of his father with dark complexion and black hair, while Ned and Harriet were both fair-skinned and blonde. He told me later that he never suspected a thing. But that is how men are, isn't it?" She laughed briefly but it was without mirth.

"Marvin was soon offered a job back east in his family's business. He talked it over with me and we decided that this might be the perfect solution. We would get married and move far away from Felix. In the back of my mind always was Charlie. But I was so unsure of what Marvin's response would be to the fact that I had a son. He had made it clear to me that he was in no hurry to have kids. And I knew how much Ned and Harriet loved him and that he was safe and secure with them. One day I stopped by their home and explained the situation to them. They offered to keep him for as long as I needed. I had no idea how long that would become."

"We moved to Ohio and started a new life. Susan and Michael came along after a few years, and then, you, Janet. We were so happy. My life in California became like...well, like a dream. And then, one day, I received a letter from Harriet. I can remember it like it was yesterday," her eyes grew moist once again.

"In this letter, the letter you found, Abby," she pointed to the letter laying on the coffee table, "she mentioned that Charlie was going to be six on his next birthday and that they were tired of living in limbo. She also mentioned that Felix was out of the picture.

I wasn't sure what she meant so I called her later that week. She told me that she had heard from a woman at church who knew his aunt that Felix had been killed in a bar fight. It was a sad ending to a sadder life," she murmured and then went on, "I knew I had to finally tell Marvin about Charlie. And so we sat down one night after the kids were in bed and I told him everything. We talked and prayed and then talked some more. In the end, we decided that, if Ned and Harriet were willing, we'd ask them to adopt Charlie permanently. It just seemed to be in his best interest."

She looked up to answer the unspoken question in both of their eyes.

"I know you think I must have been a horrible mother to desert Charlie like that. And I know I was. But it wasn't that I didn't love Charlie. I always have. I always will. I only wanted to do what was best for my boy. Ned and Harriet were wonderful God-fearing people and loved Charlie as their own. In the end, we decided to never talk about it again," she explained further, "That's how things were in those days. You just didn't talk about things like you do today."

The story was an age-old story and nothing new. Both Janet and Abby knew that it happened over and over to innocent, starry-eyed young women who fell prey to handsome, abusive men. They just never dreamed such a thing had happened to their dear mother and grandmother.

Belinda continued, "In the end, we decided it would be a secret between just us four. Even Charlie never knew. Eventually, we lost touch with them, being so far away and all. Harriet sent me a few photos through the years but, eventually, even those stopped."

She stopped and sat quietly for a few minutes, unsure how to continue. Finally, she said quietly, "And so I just lived my life like Charlie didn't exist. But, always, in my heart, is an empty Charlie-shaped space. I loved Charlie dearly and it was a great sacrifice to give him up. I still love him," she said softly and then looked up, "and that's the story."

The three of them all just sat quietly, unsure of what to say upon this revelation. The silence remained unbroken until Abby's father came in from the garage and stood in the doorway, "My goodness, I don't think I've ever seen the three of you this quiet in all my days," he joked.

They turned serious eyes upon him. It was Janet who spoke up, "Mom's been filling us in on her big secret."

Tom raised his eyebrows and then wisely returned to the garage but his entrance had broken the silence.

"Thank you, Mom, for telling me that. I truly had no idea," said Janet, still reeling from this unexpected confession of her mother's.

Abby realized, maybe for the first time in her life, that her grandmother was an actual person. She had hopes, dreams, fears, and, yes, even sins—just like everybody else.

It was Janet who suggested they pray. They prayed for the situation. They prayed for Charlie. They prayed for her grandmother.

As they prayed an idea began to form in Abby's mind. As it grew, she began to grow excited. She would find Charlie for Grandma! She would find him by Christmas. She smiled broadly to herself as her mother continued to pray.

John and Abby pulled up next to an old home. One half was painted a grayish blue. The other half was a dingy white. Abby looked at the numbers. She was going to the blue half.

"Ok, I'll be right back."

"You are sure you don't want me to come with you?"

"I just think it would be better to not overwhelm him. Going alone seems wisest."

John nodded and then gave a small wave, pulling his phone out of his pocket to check on what was happening in the sports world.

Abby noticed the well-maintained little yard and the happy little snowman on the painted porch. Soon she was at the door.

She took a deep breath and knocked. As she waited, she reflected on how she had ended up knocking on the front door of this sweet little home.

She had never dreamed how hard it would be to find her uncle. Charles Clark was apparently a very common name. The fact that Ned and Harriet Clark had moved overseas at some point really complicated things. The fact that none of the family were anywhere to be found on social media complicated things even further.

Finally, after weeks of searching and talking to what felt like dozens of *Charles Clarks,* she had found a Charles Clark that lived in this little half house in a suburb of Kansas City. His kind voice had responded to her questions. Yes, his parents were Ned and Harriet.

Yes, he had two younger sisters named Pam and Beth. As the conversation marched on it became very evident that she had finally found Uncle Charlie!

Abby had broached the subject very carefully but she had had nothing to fear. He was aware of his adoption and had actually been planning to search for his biological mother after the holidays. It had taken him long enough to find her already but "life had always gotten in the way" as he had put it.

He went on to talk about his busy life as a plumber and the four kids he and his late wife, Nancy, had had. Uncle Charlie was a delight to talk to, inserting humor into the conversation but also talking seriously when the occasion arose. He was actively involved in his local Baptist church and oversaw the widow/widower ministry there.

Providentially, John already had a business trip planned in the Kansas City area in the near future. Abby couldn't help but believe this was a God-given opportunity and so she asked him if she could stop by for a visit, which he had warmly welcomed.

That had been about a month ago. And this is what brought her to his door today. She was hoping to convince him to meet Grandma for Christmas.

Wouldn't that be the most awesome Christmas present ever? She thought excitedly as she waited.

After a few very long minutes, her knock was answered. There stood a woman about her age with short blond hair. She had dark circles under her eyes and looked exhausted.

Abby cleared her throat in her surprise, looking down at her phone to confirm the house number, and then nervously started to speak, "I...um...I'm sorry. I must have the wrong house. I was looking for Charlie Clark."

The woman sighed, "You have the right house. You must be Abby. Dad told me you were coming, although he never did tell me when. Come on in."

Abby looked out at the car where John was watching. She subtly shrugged her shoulders at him and then followed the woman inside.

As she walked into the front room, it was full of boxes and containers. Photos and artwork had been removed from the walls and had been carefully placed on the coffee table. Knick-knacks were piled high on the table that Abby could see in the next room. The tired woman offered her a seat on a comfortable sofa covered with muted blue flowers.

"Oh, Abby," she gave a tired smile, "I feel like I know you already. Dad was so thrilled to talk to you. You just have no idea."

Abby's hopes started to fade. Something was very wrong. She didn't have to wait long to find out what.

"A few days after he talked to you, Dad had a massive heart attack. It must have happened during the night. My sister found him the next morning. She had stopped by when he hadn't answered her phone call," The words were said robotically, as if she had repeated them many times.

She continued, "I am so very sorry, Abby. He was so very excited to meet you and, particularly, to meet his biological mother. It had taken him so many years to finally start the search. Both Grandpa and Grandma had blessed his search and had given him what they knew about his mother—which, of course, is your grandma. I am not sure what was going on inside him, as he tended to not speak too often of his feelings, but there was something in the past year that was driving him on his search. He was planning to reach out after Christmas," she said the words sadly.

Abby sat there, stunned and deeply disappointed. She mourned the uncle she would never really know. It was almost made worse by the fact that she had talked to him and they had hit it off so well.

"I guess I should introduce myself. I am Shelly, Charlie's youngest daughter. I am working on cleaning out the house and getting it ready to sell. It all feels... surreal," her eyes looked around at all of the mess.

"I am so sorry you have lost your father. How awful! I can't even imagine," Suddenly, Abby realized that Shelly's loss was far greater than hers.

Shelly sighed deeply, "it is. And it was so unexpected. Dad was in such good health."

They sat there awkwardly for a minute or two. There seemed to be little else to say, under the circumstances.

Finally, Shelly broke the silence, "I guess, officially, we are cousins..."

Abby smiled brightly at that, "Yes, I guess that's true. Very nice to meet you, cousin."

Shelly continued, "I know my sisters and brother would love to meet you but this may not be the best time. My sister, Lori—the one who found him—isn't handling this well at all. She's been really struggling."

Abby's brow grew concerned as she said "Oh, I totally understand."

The two women made arrangements to stay in touch and to perhaps meet at a later time and then stood up. As Abby made her way to the front door, she heard Shelly say, "Wait!"

She turned around and she could see Shelly digging around in one of the boxes. From it she pulled a family photo in a wooden frame. She then went to another box and pulled out a tiny, porcelain angel.

"Can you give these to your grandma? This will show her dad's family," she held up the frame and then gave a brief description of everyone in the photo. Abby hoped she would remember.

"And this," she said, holding up the tiny angel, "meant a lot to dad and I want your grandma to have it." She went on to explain that most of the abundant knick-knacks they were busily packing away were her mother's but that this tiny angel had been a gift to dad during her mother's battle with cancer and he had treasured it.

"I was planning to keep it but it just seems right that your grandma should have it."

"Thank you so much. I know this will mean the world to her."

Abby reached her arms out to Shelly and gave her a warm hug. They had met as strangers but were parting as family.

John was waiting anxiously and was relieved when Abby opened the car door.

"Well...?"

Sorrow filled Abby's eyes, "Oh, John. It won't be the Christmas I had hoped for, after all."

Christmas dawned bright and clear. The kids were jumping on the bed by 7am, excited about their gifts. John and Abby groaned playfully as the kids begged to open presents. After a wonderful, chaotic, and loud morning, they got ready to go to Abby's parents' house for Christmas dinner.

It was around noon when they pulled out of their driveway. Abby's mind went yet again, as it so often had over the past few weeks, to the disappointment of Uncle Charlie not being there this Christmas.

Grandma had taken it pretty well, overall. She had been pretty shaken up by the whole thing but was somewhat comforted by the fact that he had been actively walking with the Lord, which meant she would see him again one day.

Abby was not so comforted. She had felt a real connection with him upon their phone conversation and her disappointment was profound. She knew he would have fit into their family so perfectly. Why had God allowed him to die at such a horrible time??

She gave an imperceptible shake of her head, as if to rid it of unwanted thoughts. Today was no day to be having these maudlin thoughts. And she certainly knew she shouldn't be questioning God's sovereignty. Sometimes that was hard, though.

The kids started singing *Jingle Bells* in the back seat and John soon joined in. Abby left her depressing thoughts behind on this lovely Christmas Day and joined in, as well.

Soon they were all piling into Grandpa and Grandma's house with joyous shouts of "Merry Christmas!" and lots of hugs. Grandma Belinda sat smiling in the recliner, hugging anyone who came over to wish her a Merry Christmas.

Tom and Janet smiled joyfully as the house began to fill up with Abby's family and the families of her two brothers.

The delicious smell of baked ham wafted through the air and pies, cakes, and cookies sat on the counter. Abby laughed to herself. Mom always did cook for an army. She knew they'd put away containers and containers of leftovers, just like they did every year.

Tom thanked the Lord for the meal and the family began to eat. Suddenly, the doorbell rang.

"Now who could that be?" said Janet, wonderingly.

Tom glanced her way as he spooned a large portion of mashed potatoes on to his plate, "I have no idea."

Janet got up from her place at the table to go answer the door.

When she opened the door there stood three strangers, smiling.

"Merry Christmas!" They exclaimed.

"I am Shelly..." said the woman with the short, blond hair.

When Abby heard the familiar voice she hurried to join her mother.

"Shelly! What in the world are you doing here?" She said with a huge smile.

Janet looked questioningly at Abby.

"Mom, I'd like to officially introduce you to your niece, Shelly."

"Oh, my goodness! How wonderful to meet you!"

"This is my husband, Shawn," she pointed to the tall, thin man that stood smiling by her side and then, pointing to the woman with long brown hair who looked very much like a younger Grandma Belinda, "this is my sister, Lori."

"Oh, come in, come in. Please!"

Belinda sat quietly eating at the table, not realizing that two of her granddaughters had stopped by for a visit.

Janet brought the two women over to the table and said, "Mom, I'd like you to meet Shelly and Lori. These are two of Charlie's girls."

Belinda's eyes grew wide and she was speechless in her delight.

They quickly added an extra leaf to the table and retrieved some extra folding chairs from the closet. Cooking for an army had served Janet well on this occasion and they enjoyed a wonderful Christmas dinner together.

After everyone was filled to the brim with the delicious holiday home-cooked meal, they went into the large family room. Sending the kids down to the basement to play for a bit, the adults sat and talked. Shelly explained how they had happened to come there on Christmas day.

"After Abby called dad, it became his dearest held plan to come and see you after the holidays. I had never seen him so excited. A few weeks after he died, us kids talked about perhaps continuing his plan. We knew it would never be the same as meeting your own son," she directed this to Grandma Belinda, "but we wanted to fill in this missing piece to our family puzzle.

A few weeks before Christmas Lori and I realized that neither of us had anything special planned over the holidays. Shawn and I don't have any kids...yet," she added the *yet* with a glimmer of hope in her eyes, "and Lori's two boys are with their father this weekend. Instead of staying home and mourning dad over the holidays, we thought, why not go meet our grandmother at Christmastime?

We were going to call in advance, but then started thinking how fun it would be to surprise you. Abby had given every indication that you would welcome us and so we decided to take a chance and here we are!" she laughed.

Belinda's heart was full, "Oh, how I would have loved to meet your father. It would have been my greatest gift ever!" but then she continued on, smiling broadly at her two granddaughters, "but having you girls here today—why, it's just so very wonderful!"

"Jessie and Kevin want to meet you sometime, too," said Lori, referring to their other two siblings, "But they have families and so much going on over the holidays so they just could not come along today," and then she told Grandma Belinda a little bit about her other two grandchildren that she had yet to meet.

Abby watched them all talk and laugh and thought about how comfortable it all felt. The cousins she had never met already felt like family within a few short hours. She sighed with contentment.

No, this Christmas had certainly not turned out how she had dreamed. In what felt far too early, Charlie had left this old earth for his permanent home in heaven. A home that is only for those who recognize their lost and sinful state before God and their utter helplessness in being right with Him and, in that helplessness, turn to Christ alone for salvation (see *John 3:16; John 14:6*).

All at once, Abby realized just how much hope and comfort this truth really did give. How kind of God to assure Grandma that, even if not in this life, she would see Charlie in the next.

And then Abby thought of God's goodness in bringing her two cousins to their door today. Oh, how wonderful for them to surprise Grandma. Amazingly, there was no awkwardness. Both Lori and Shelly, and her husband, too, fit in like they had always been part of the family.

Janet came and sat next to Abby and touched her arm, "Thank you," she said, her eyes bright with unshed tears.

Abby smiled and hugged her mom. No, this Christmas wasn't anything like she expected but it was a wonderful Christmas, nonetheless.

Christmas at the Cabin

"Gianna, your dad will soon be here."

Gianna rolled her eyes at her mom as she dropped her suitcase by the door. If Mallory was honest, she felt the same way her daughter did. She didn't really want the girls to go to their dad's house for this weekend before Christmas but she had to do what was right, even if the kids didn't like the girlfriend that had stolen him away from the family. It was hard to understand how someone who claimed to be a Christian could just leave his family without even a glance back. It had been over a year and she still wasn't sure she'd ever get over the shock. And she wasn't sure she could ever forgive him.

But at least they could be in the same room together now.. She just had to get through the upcoming divorce. And then they could go on to live their separate lives.

Except for the girls, of course. They would have to work together for the sake of the girls. She sighed. Sometimes the last year of pain and sorrow still seemed surreal.

In an hour, Mallory was alone. Mark and his girlfriend had picked up fifteen-year-old Gianna and thirteen-year-old Gemma and driven away, leaving her to spend the entire weekend alone. She always dreaded these weekends.

134

As Mallory was sadly wondering what she was going to do all weekend, her daughters were feverishly texting each other in the backseat of the car.

What's wrong with Dad? texted Gemma.

A shrugging shoulders emoji was the response.

Crystal is awful quiet. Do you think they had a fight? came the next text.

Maybe? Suddenly, Gianna's face lit up with hope and she texted: *Maybe they are going to break up?*

Gemma smiled knowingly at Gianna. They had never given up hope of their parents getting back together.

Mark glanced at them in the backseat and asked, "What would you girls think about going to the cabin for the weekend?"

Crystal gave a deep, disgusted sigh.

Mark ignored her.

"That sounds great, Dad!"

"Awesome!" They responded at the same time.

Crystal coolly glanced at the girls and then glared at Mark, "I told you I can't go this weekend. Nor do I want to. You don't even have cell signal at that cabin. And it's so boring there," she complained.

The girls waited with bated breath to see what would happen. To have their father to themselves for the whole weekend would be like a dream.

They soon realized that they would get their wish when their father pulled up to Crystal's house, dropped her off, and told her aloofly that he'd see her next week. She slammed the car door and stomped away.

Soon they were on their way to their father's apartment. There, he grabbed what he would need for the weekend. He texted Mallory, knowing how much she loved the cabin, and invited her to come and pick up the girls there, if she'd like. Otherwise, he'd bring them back on Sunday evening. Mallory agreed as the cabin by the creek in the woods was one of her favorite places in the whole world. She'd go up for the day on

Sunday and have the kids home in time to go to school on Monday.

While she didn't relish the idea of spending the day with Crystal, being at that peaceful place in the woods would be worth a bit of awkwardness.

Soon Mark and his daughters were taking the two-hour trip north to the cabin. As they climbed up through the mountains, they had a wonderful time talking and laughing and singing. For the first time in a long time, their father seemed like his old self.

Gemma finally just had to ask, "Dad, why can't we laugh and sing like this when Crystal is around?"

Mark gave a disillusioned sighed, "you know, I am not sure. But the more I get to know her the more I am realizing that she is not the one for me."

"Really?" Gianna questioned, hope filling her heart.

"I hate to say it, but, yes. She's just too stuck up for me. Really no fun at all," Mark laughed.

What he didn't say to his girls was that God was really working on his heart. He had been drawn back to church and had begun a Bible Study with an older man there. This man, Darryl, had been faithful to his wife for over fifty years and showed the rewards and vibrancy of a life lived unashamedly for God. Mark was beginning to believe he made a huge mistake by leaving his family.

But he didn't tell this to his daughters. It was too new. Too soon.

But his heart was beginning to soften. God was beginning the marvelous work of restoration that only He can accomplish in a man's heart.

Meanwhile, Mallory spent a lot of time with God that lonely weekend. She pulled out the Bible Study that she had cast aside in the past few busy weeks and decided to spend some really quality time in the Word.

Through this dedicated time, God convicted her of the bitterness that had grown up in her heart like a cancer. She had really struggled to forgive Mark. She knew that. But she did not realize just how it was affecting her relationship with God and even affecting the girls.

Until that solitary weekend when God so lovingly and kindly opened her eyes.

The Mallory that traveled north on Sunday was a different Mallory than the one who had bid her husband and daughters good-bye on Friday evening. She felt free for the first time since Mark had left.

"Everything seems new and bright and beautiful," she thought as she traveled under the sparkling blue sky and bright winter sun.

It's amazing how forgiveness can change a heart and mind.

Mark and the girls were in the front yard throwing a frisbee as they waited for Mallory to arrive. It had been a wonderful weekend. The best they had had since the family had separated.

The girls didn't realize that Mark was under terrible conviction about his own selfishness in walking away from his family and that he was working to right his relationship with his daughters. All they knew was that it almost seemed as if they had their old dad back. The one that loved them unconditionally and had had devotions with them and had tucked them lovingly in at night. They both blossomed under their father's love.

As is the case with most split families, the girls had not gone unharmed. Gianna had started hanging out with the wrong crowd and Gemma was struggling with her school grades. But none of that mattered this weekend. This weekend they were reminded that their dad loved them. And that was all that mattered for the moment.

As Mallory's black jeep pulled into the driveway, she saw the three standing there together. Mark's arms were around the girls and they all looked so happy together.

Where is Crystal? She wondered. She didn't have to wait long to find out.

"Hi, Mom!" the girls gathered around her with warm hugs and happy faces. Mallory glanced at Mark. His face was the happiest and carefree she'd seen in a very long time. What was going on?

Mark jogged over and smiled warmly at her, "Want to join us for lunch? Or did you eat?"

"Sure, I'd love to. I haven't eaten yet." Where *was* Crystal? Preparing lunch?

But, no, she wasn't in the house either. In fact, not only was she not there but neither were any of her things.

Finally, she whispered to Gianna, "Where's Crystal?"

Gianna gave her a broad smile as she said happily, "she didn't come!"

This was the first time it had been just the four of them together for a meal since Mark had left. Mallory's heart beat a bit faster as she realized this and she prepared herself for it to be very awkward.

But it wasn't. In fact, it wasn't at all. Mark was at ease and especially kind. Sandwiches and fruit and chips were eaten with much laughter and light-hearted conversation.

"Wow! Would you look at that?" shouted Gemma.

She pulled back the curtain to show the snow that was falling fast and furiously.

Mallory looked worriedly at Mark, "Were they calling for snow?"

"Not that I knew of," he said and then added, "But why don't we enjoy it?" He said and, smiling, he grabbed a Christmas puzzle from a nearby shelf, persuading them all to join him at the table.

Mallory went into the kitchen and made some hot cocoa from the packets they kept in the pantry and brought the steaming cups into the dining room.

The next couple hours found them all pouring over the puzzle together like old times. In those two hours, Mark's heart continued to soften towards his family.

And then there was the moment when Mallory shouted in glee over a found piece of the puzzle that she had been searching for and he realized, quite suddenly, that he still loved his wife.

He shook his head imperceptibly. Maybe it was just the situation playing with his emotions. He knew he had to be sure. He didn't want to play with the hearts of his family.

But as the snow continued to fall and the family reunited over cocoa and puzzles and games, the feeling of love in his heart only grew.

He found himself comparing Crystal to Mallory and he had to admit that Crystal was found wanting. Where Crystal would have only complained about being snowed in, Mallory viewed it as an opportunity. Where Crystal would have complained over not having her specialty coffee, Mallory licked her lips in satisfaction over cocoa made from an out-of-date packet. Where Crystal would have complained about no cell service, Mallory viewed it as a wonderful challenge to keep themselves occupied in the old-fashioned way.

Yes, there was no comparison, Mark realized as the evening wore on. He had given up his wonderful family for a complaining shrew of a woman.

As Mallory and the girls prepared supper, he went over to the window to watch the snow fall. As it made its way down, he realized they were going to be there for more than a couple of days. And, all of a sudden, he realized this for the unexpected opportunity that it was. Could he win back his family? He knew he had to try.

It was Christmas Eve. The prior three days had been wonderful for the little family. The whole world had faded away and all that was left was the four of them in this special place.

Thankfully, Mark had restocked the pantry the month before and they had plenty of canned goods for their meals. It wasn't ideal, but none of them seemed to mind.

They had spent the past few days playing games, putting puzzles together, making snow angels, and having snowball fights.

Each one of them, deep down in their hearts, wanted this week to go on forever. None of them were in a hurry for the snow plow to come and plow them out.

As in the old days, they decided to open gifts on Christmas Eve. They were unable to go to the store, so they had to find and use things that were already in the cabin.

The homemade gifts were placed carefully under the small tree that Mark and the girls had put up the weekend before.

Gianna handed out her gifts first. She had written letters, letting each person know how much she appreciated them and why. There were few dry eyes as they read the special letters.

Next, Gemma handed out her gifts. She loved origami and, finding some old construction paper, she had carefully crafted a flower for her sister, a beautiful bird for her mom, and a bear for her dad.

"Oh, these are so lovely," exclaimed Mallory.

"These are amazing! What a talented daughter I have," said Mark.

Gemma glowed at these words of praise.

Mallory smiled at the girls as she handed out her gifts. She had been excited when she remembered that the Christmas gifts from her recent shopping trip were still in the back of her jeep. She had dug through the bags and found the small boxes she was searching for. She wrapped them with paper she found in the desk drawer, adding brightly colored stickers still around from when the girls were little.

The girls carefully unwrapped their gifts to find the blue velvet boxes. As they lifted the lid, they found a gold necklace with a small diamond-studded heart.

"Oh, it's beautiful, Mom!" cried the girls in unison.

"You like it? I am so glad! These will remind you that you are always loved, no matter what. By God and by me and by your father, too," she said, glancing at him.

And then she hesitantly handed a small box to Mark. "What is this?"

"It's for you. I brought it along this weekend and was planning to give it to you."

He opened it to find his wedding ring.

"I realize that I can't hang on to *us* anymore," she hesitantly began and then took a deep breath and continued, "I must let you live your own life. You have been with Crystal for a long time and it's time that I forgive you and give both of us the freedom to move on.

And I do forgive you, Mark. Only by the grace and power of God, can I forgive you. But God has worked mightily in my heart and I can honestly say that I forgive you now. So, there," she picked up the box that he had set down on the coffee table and held it out to him, "Take the ring and go live your life. I wish you the best. I really do mean that," Mallory's voice thickened as she said the last line. She still loved him so much. The words were much harder to say than she had expected.

Mark just stared at the ring in his hands. He realized that he didn't want his freedom. He didn't want the divorce that he had been so passionate to have just a short time ago. What had changed?

He looked up and observed the lovely faces before him. First, Gianna, with her straight blonde hair and blue eyes, so much like his own; and then Gemma, the spitting image of her mama with her auburn hair and deep brown eyes; and then he turned to Mallory. He soaked in her loveliness and considered her kind-heartedness and positive attitude. He knew that her little speech had taken great fortitude and courage.

"What if I've changed my mind?" He didn't plan to say it. But there it was. It was what he was thinking and it came out of his lips before he had a chance to stop it.

"Wwwhat..?" Mallory stammered.

Their daughters looked at each other in disbelieving delight. Had they heard their father correctly?

He had said it and he wasn't going to back down now, "What if I don't want us to be over? I've been such an idiot. I know that now. The Lord knows it has taken me long enough but He never gave up on me. I know it would take a lot of work. It won't be a fairy tale to try to rebuild our marriage. And it won't be 'happily ever after' like it is in the movies. But I'd really like to try again. What do you say?" He glanced eagerly at his wife. At his family.

Tears began to spill out of Mallory's eyes. She had wanted this so badly for so long. Did she still want it? Was she brave enough to try? Could she trust him?

In this unexpected moment, she didn't really know.

"Can I think about it?" she said quietly.

"Of course." Mark responded tersely, rejection washing over him.

The girls' smiles turned into surprised frowns as they heard their mom's response.

Mark's heart hurt as he faced what he knew he deserved. Mallory had no reason to trust him. None whatsoever. Oh, what had he done? How he mourned his foolishness.

The rest of the evening passed by in an awkwardness that was uncomfortable. The elephant in the room stood there, demanding attention. But it was soundly ignored as the hours ticked by until, finally, they could retreat to their beds.

Mallory awoke to the sun shining brightly through her curtains. She sleepily crawled out of bed to look out the window. She saw the snow plow finally coming up the lane.

She could go home today. She wasn't sure if that thought made her happy or sad.

She donned the old sweats and sweatshirt that had been at the cabin and which she had worn most of the week and then quietly headed downstairs to make coffee.

Mark was already at the kitchen table, staring out the window with a cup of black coffee in his hand.

"I'm sorry," he said as she poured a cup for herself and then sat down.

"I'm just so sorry. I've been such a fool. I can see that now," His eyes filled with tears.

Mallory stared at him. Mark didn't cry. Ever. And he was terrible at acting. Did this mean he was genuine in what he was saying? Could she trust him to be sincere?

Mark went on to share his heart with Mallory. He explained, without using the all-too-familiar excuses, about his choices and why he may have made them. It was the first time they had honestly discussed what had happened without him, even once, defending himself.

Mallory responded with love and also apologized for her part in their failed marriage.

Finally, Mark ended by saying, "the bottom line is that I followed my lusts and chose very purposefully to walk away from not only my family but also from the Lord. It took me way too long to understand this. But God, in His great grace and mercy, has opened my eyes to my sin. I know you say you have forgiven me but I want you to know that I know that I need your forgiveness. And I thank you for it, no matter where we go from here."

Mallory stared at the table and sighed. And then, eyes shining from unshed tears, she turned to look at him and said, "I do still love you, you know."

Mark took a deep breath, "I was hoping you'd say that," he paused before continuing, "What do you say? Can we try again? Please? Can we piece our marriage back together with God's help? We've ignored Him and His Word far too long in our marriage and in our home. Can we try a second time with Him at the center of our lives?"

Mallory got up from the table and went to where Mark sat. He stood up and gazed into her eyes.

"Yes. I want to try," she said.

Mark took her in his arms and, for the first time in a long time, Mallory believed that everything was going to be okay. Not *easy* but okay.

The girls crept down the stairs, and upon hearing conversation in the kitchen they sat quietly listening to their parents. When the conversation stopped they quietly peeked around the corner and saw their parents embracing one another. They gave squeals of joy.

"Yay! Oh, Yay! God, thank you!" they shouted as they jumped up and down.

Three months later

Gianna and Gemma got off the bus and walked into the house to find their parents hugging.

"Really?" teased Gianna, giving a big eye roll.

"Gross," said Gemma with laughter in her voice.

The past three months hadn't been easy. It had been messy and difficult to repair what had been so wrong in their marriage but Mark and Mallory were both committed. They were working together to rebuild their life together.

Darryl, Mark's mentor, and his wife, Martha, had come alongside them and were helping them understand what scripture said about marriage, setting a wonderful example of what they taught by their own marriage. Mark and Mallory understood that submission and obedience to scripture would yield the healthiest and most blessed of marriages.

Eventually, the broken marriage was healed and the hurting family transformed. God had changed a life and had softened a hard heart, as only He can do.

No one is ever too far gone for God.

Note from the Author

All of the stories contained in this book, with the exception of *Christmas at the Cabin*, were originally published at *growing4life.net*. I created the blog in 2010 but it wasn't until the fall of 2016 that I had the idea of writing an original Christmas story. I divided the story into five parts and presented it weekly throughout the month of December. I enjoyed writing something a bit different and my readers seemed to enjoy the stories. And that's how the *Growing4Life* Christmas story tradition came to be.

A few years ago, I thought about compiling these stories into a little book. It took me until this year to actually make it happen.

I like to read these kinds of pleasant stories at Christmas time. Who doesn't love a happy ending?

Unfortunately, many of us do not get a fairy tale ending to our own personal stories. Soldiers don't always return from the battlefield; family members remain estranged for life; marriages splinter and break, never to be put back together. Life is full of hurts and woes.

But, no matter what your life story, be it happy or sad, hard or easy, there is one thing of which you can be sure: *God loves you.*

You will have noticed that many of these stories have a religious component to them. But I want to assure you that it isn't just any religion.

The Baby in a manger that we sing about at Christmastime is God, very God who came to dwell with mankind in order to save us from our sins. He would go on to die on the cross and then rise again, to live and reign forever. Only He can save us from our sins and give us everlasting life.

Today, there are many counterfeits that go by the name of "Jesus". But there is only <u>one true Jesus</u>.

If you'd like to get to know the real Jesus, may I suggest you turn to the book of John in the Bible and start reading. That is a great place to get started for anyone who really desires to understand who Jesus really is and why it matters.

It is my hope and prayer that God will use these stories to plant seeds of the Gospel in your heart if you don't know Jesus Christ.

And for those of you who already have a personal relationship with Christ, I hope these stories have encouraged your heart and have pleasantly recharged you in a busy season.

I wish you all a very, Merry Christmas! May we remember that Jesus truly is the only reason for the season!

Leslie Allebach
November, 2022

www.ingramcontent.com/pod-product-compliance
Lightning Source LLC
Chambersburg PA
CBHW052004220626
47052CB00004B/1083